On the Edge of Twilight: 22 Tales to Follow You Home

Gregory Miller

Illustrated by John Randall York

For Carol!
With deep gratitude for
all your support + enthusiasm.
I hope you like this one!
From your old teacher,
Greg Miller
PITTSBURGH
9-2012

Stonegarden.net Publishing
http://www.stonegarden.net

Reading from a different angle.
California, USA

On the Edge of Twilight: 22 Tales to Follow You Home

ISBN: 1-60076-341-3

This is a work of fiction. Names, characters, places and incidents are products of the author's imagination or are used fictitiously and are not to be construed as real. Any resemblance to actual events, locales, organizations or persons, living or dead, is entirely coincidental.

StoneGarden.net Publishing
3851 Cottonwood Dr.
Danville, CA 94506

First StoneGarden.net Publishing paperback printing:
August 2012

First StoneGarden.net Publishing electronic printing:
August 2012

Visit StoneGarden.net Publishing on the web at
http://www.stonegarden.net.

Cover art and design by John Randall York

On the Edge of Twilight:
22 Tales to Follow You Home

Table of Contents

Praise for Gregory Miller

"Gregory Miller is a fresh new talent with a great future."
--Ray Bradbury

"Gregory Miller's prose has a luminous clarity rarely seen in a postmodern age where mysterious opacity is often touted as a virtue…He addresses the reader in a poetic language that is translucent, heartfelt, and wise."
--Roderick Clark, Editor/Publisher of *Rosebud Magazine*

"The small town life depicted in *The Uncanny Valley* is in many ways familiar and comfortable territory, but each story demonstrates that something unnatural lurks beneath the surface. As the stories coalesce to form a larger narrative, the perversity builds…On its own, each individual anecdote is merely curious; as a collective, they become morbidly sinister."
--Booksellers Without Borders

"Miller's intriguing premise and incredibly creative stories had me completely enthralled…one of the best eerie books I've read."
--*Book Matters*, reviewing *The Uncanny Valley*

"[*The Uncanny Valley*] is an inspired and original idea, breathing fresh life into a popular and revered genre."
--Novelist and critic Daniel Cann

"Gregory Miller's tales in *Scaring the Crows* are wonderfully dark, wonderfully various, and wonderfully wrought."
--Brad Strickland, award-winning author of the *Grimoire* series.

"*Scaring the Crows* is a delightful collection. The stories are chock full of heart and description, and you're left amazed that you could grow so attached to the quirky and often quite likeable characters in such bite-sized works."
--*Hawleyville Reviews*

"It's easy to imagine [*Scaring the Crows*] being done by one of the old greats… This book is a treat."
--*Book Reviews Weekly*

Other StoneGarden.net Publishing titles by Gregory Miller

Scaring the Crows: 21 Tales for Noon or Midnight

The Uncanny Valley: Tales from a Lost Town

In Memory of Ray Bradbury:
Mentor,
Teacher,
Friend,
with “love to the end of the 21st century.”

And for Zee, always and forever my Big Sis.

Acknowledgements

These stories were first published in the following venues, and are reprinted with permission:

"The Forest and the Trees," "Time to Go Home," "The Leasehold of His Days," and "Supper-Time" in *The Sounding of the Sea: Five Tales of Loss and Redemption.* Lame Goat Press, 2010.

"The Saver" in *Potter's Field 4.* Sam's Dot Publishing, 2011.

"Shells" in *Three Stories (Vol. 1, No. 2).* OmicronWorld Entertainment, 2009.

"Par One" and "A Quick Break" in *Flash!* Static Movement, 2010.

"The Subject" in *Halloween Frights II.* Static Movement, 2011.

"The Return" in *Cup of Joe: Coffee House Flash.* Wicked East Press, 2011.

"The Key" in *Caught by Darkness.* Static Movement, 2010.

"Miss Riley's Lot" in *Day Terrors.* The Harrow Press, 2011.

"Wood Smoke" in *Don't Tread on Me: Tales of Revenge and Retribution.* Static Movement, 2010.

All other stories are original to this collection.

Finally, many thanks to Laury Egan and Tracy Fabre, for their thoughtful and painstaking editorial work and suggestions.

Time held me green and dying
Though I sang in my chains like the sea.

—Dylan Thomas

Houses are not haunted. ***We*** *are haunted.*

—Dean Koontz

The Forest and the Trees

An abundance of forest borders Still Creek, but the small expanse of Still Creek Wood stands alone on the hill above my grandparents' house. When I was young, Grandpa and I walked it every time I visited, even the last Christmas before he died, when he knew his heart was almost kaput and that any kind of outdoor walking was full of risk.

Unlike other forests that fringe town, there is never any trash in those woods, and hunters shy away from them. So Grandpa, who spent his youth working underground in the coal mines and his middle age teaching in classrooms, liked it up there, beneath the rustle of leaves and the sigh of branches. I've almost forgotten what that feels like: to be at ease in a quiet place you know is safe.

But it wasn't always safe.

Four months after Grandpa died, in early May, right after my tenth birthday, Grandma sat me down with a piece of pumpkin pie and a glass of milk.

"Promise me you won't go in the forest behind the house anymore," she said. "Promise me you'll leave Still Creek Wood well enough alone."

I was surprised. "But I go in there all the time! And it's the easiest way to get to the top of Still Creek Hill and over to the fairgrounds."

Grandma stood firm. "That may be, Dennis, but it isn't safe without your Grandpa. When you're older, maybe I'll explain."

"Why not now? Why not for sure?"

"Just promise me. There are plenty of other places around here for a boy to explore."

Well, I promised, even though I didn't understand why. But I was ten, and I was told not to do something for my own good. What choice did I have? On the final day of the visit, hours before Mom and I started the three-hour drive home, she and Grandma went to Plumville to shop for crafts, and I stayed behind and did what I promised not to do.

I trotted up the back yard, past the flower garden under the maple tree, the flagstone walk, and the tool shed; past the burn pile, the three pine trees, and the old stone spring, until the long, wet grass of May became strewn with mildewed leaves and the forest loomed.

When I was very young, I thought there were man-made trails through Still Creek Wood, but as I got older I realized they were due to the natural placement of the trees. The trees grow tall and full without being smothered. Their branches intertwine but don't compete for sunlight or air. No one made the trails. The trees did.

I followed a familiar path. Grandpa and I used to walk to the point where the forest ends atop the hill, then over to the western edge bordering Mr. Collins' wheat field and back down to the yard. I went that way, since it made me think of Grandpa; only three months after his death, I had already come to realize the importance of routine as a method of remembering what has gone away.

For the most part the forest floor was dark, but sunlight broke through in places, and every so often I stopped to look up at the fractured rays that filtered down among the softly groaning boughs high above. I enjoyed the rustle of leaves and the noise of branches clacking gently together. Far off, I could hear the bells of the church on Pugh Street tolling the time: five o' clock.

The only evidence of human presence within the forest was (and still is, so far as I know) toward the bottom of the western edge, a couple dozen yards from Mr. Collins' field, where an old set of seven stone steps had been hauled out from an abandoned barn many years before. Whenever Grandpa and I walked in the woods, we'd always stopped by them. I don't know why they fascinated me. Maybe it was seeing stairs in a place where they didn't belong. Maybe it was seeing the stairs slowly, gradually begin to look more and more like they *did* belong, as moss, fallen leaves, and weather did their work. Regardless, they had been in the forest since before I was born, lying among the trees but not touching them, not *of* them, and I liked their strangeness.

But this time, as the angle of the falling sun sent long shadows reaching out behind all standing things, I realized something had changed.

I came to where the steps should have been… and couldn't find them. For a few unhappy moments I thought maybe someone had finally broken them up or taken them away again, but after circling the area carefully, eyes focused on the closely-patterned landscape, I suddenly realized, with a start, why I'd missed them.

The stairs now leaned against a full-grown oak tree, forty feet tall if an inch. Its straight trunk gave way to branches that arched over my head like open arms. Now the stairs rose, upright, to the lowest branch of the tree, supported by the rough, solid trunk.

I walked around the tree several times, trying to tell for sure whether I was in the right spot. Yes. A flat boulder Grandpa used to rest on still sat in its usual place amid a bed of fern just a spit away, rain-stained and covered with pale green lichen. A squat poplar still grew nearby as it always had.

My heart raced and I remember letting out a thin sigh, confronted for the first time in my life with something that didn't make sense and couldn't be explained.

Somehow, in the five months since Grandpa and I had taken our final walk together, an oak had grown from nothing to full, stately height, moving the steps with its growth until they climbed, with rediscovered purpose, to meet its boughs.

I crept over to the steps, ran my hand over the worn, moss-covered slab, and clambered up the old stone cuts. Reaching the top, I grabbed the oak's lowest branch, hoisted myself up, twisted around, and then, with a gasp and a grunt, plunked down on it.

Above and around me the leaves of the tree rustled softly. I looked about, impressed by the height and view, hardly realizing how comfortable the crook of the branch had become. And as I sat there, I gradually became aware of my own feelings: for the first time since bitter, cold February, I had allowed the preoccupations of worry and grief to fall away, lulled by the murmur of sap-blood and gently shifting leaves. The great, crushing wheel of loss had been halted, if only briefly. Security and comfort had taken its place.

A short time later the town bell tolled six. Mom and Grandma would be returning from Plumville soon. Jolted, I felt for the top of the stone with my feet, and, finding it, trotted back down the steps and broke into a jog. The back yard was close, only a hundred yards away. It would just take a minute, and I'd be home. Just one minute—

The feel of rough, hard fingers digging into my arms is one I would like very much to forget, but the memory will not fade. As I was lifted off the ground, shrieking and hollering, legs pumping the air, it flashed through my mind that Grandma had been *right* to warn me, that I should have listened, and that promises should never, ever be broken…

I remember the strong, heady smell of pine sap and the creak of the limbs that lifted me, high, high, oh, a good fifteen feet off the ground, and it wasn't long until I had thrashed my way around and finally saw what held me.

The pine tree was massive, dark, and ancient. I'd walked past it with Grandpa many times but never stopped to look close. It was one of those trees that always looks dirty, and not very good for climbing, and even kind of scary in an indefinable sort of way. But now I knew that the deepest, gloomiest part of the tree, high in the upper boughs, had never before revealed itself. I could sense it: a brooding night of death-preserving amber sap, tangles of brittle twigs, and the soft, warm egg sacs of spiders. It was a blackness palpable, a deep gulf—and, having sensed it, I knew that if I didn't free myself from those hard, creaking branches I would come to know it well, know it intimately, and that such knowledge would be enough to darken my world forever.

With a massive, desperate twist, I wrenched myself away, dropping to the ground with a *thud* that didn't break anything but left my shoulder purple, yellow and brown for weeks to come.

Freed, sobbing, I ran.

And I never explored Still Creek Wood again.

* * *

But I did go back to Grandma's. I went back often. And it was just before the Spring Break of my senior year in college that my psychology professor gave us the assignment of conducting "20 Questions" with an older relative. "If done properly it will provide an illuminating picture of how the lives of older generations differ from the adolescents you will soon be teaching yourselves," she told us. "No 'yes' and 'no' questions in this game, though. Ask open-ended questions and encourage your subject to elaborate."

So that's what I did.

Grandma was eighty-four that year. Her eyesight was beginning to fade, but she was still sharp as ever and a willing subject. I asked about her courtship with Grandpa during the '20s, about her parents, about school conditions and grading and cars and long-dead relatives, about World War II and ration books and the Great Depression, about meeting FDR during a Gettysburg speech and attending, when she was a very little girl, the last public hanging in Pittsburgh. After an hour, I'd exhausted my set of prepared questions and started to wrap things up, but she didn't make any motion to indicate we were through. Instead, she nodded at the paper and said, "There's only nineteen questions there. You still have one to go!"

I looked down at my paper in surprise, realized she was right, and sat back in my chair to think. I heard the steady breath of spring wind as it rattled the kitchen windowpanes. Listening harder, I noted the distant sigh of branches. "Tell me why Still Creek Wood is dangerous," I said abruptly. "Tell me why I shouldn't go there."

Grandma glanced up sharply. For a moment her fingers tightened their grip on the armrests of her chair, then slowly, slowly relaxed again.

"It isn't something people speak much about," she said.

"I understand," I said quickly, embarrassed. "We don't have to talk about it. I shouldn't have said—"

Grandma threw her arms up with a great sigh. "Oh, of course you should have. You're an inquisitive soul like your Grandpa and, if I do say so myself, like me. It's in the blood. And you have a right to know, as I see it, even if you don't live in town."

Something burned behind Grandma's rheumy eyes: a knowledge that had grown ripe for imparting.

"Have you ever noticed," she asked, "how those woods are never touched by loggers?"

"I guess I figured the trees were protected. You know, by the town board or something."

"But no trash? No vandalism, no hunters? State-protected wilderness isn't well guarded, kiddo. Not in places like this."

I thought about it for a moment, realized she was right, and said so.

"All these years, the town filled with trouble-seeking boys, vandal teens, and no-good adults, and Still Creek Wood never became a club house for any of them," Grandma continued.

"So why not?" I asked.

"Because the trees protect themselves," she said simply.

And I nodded, because I knew it was so.

* * *

Like a wave held back since that long-ago day when Grandpa's loss was fresh, childhood still slipping away as the true nature of death sank in, I told Grandma everything I remembered, much of it feeling like an old half-recalled dream until my words made it real again.

And, finishing some time later, I looked up to see Grandma's cheeks were wet.

"Oh, child," she said. "You should have listened. You should have stayed away."

"Tell me why," I said. "Make me understand."

Grandma sipped gingerly at her iced tea, heeding the cold, and said, "A fair number of old folks like me know what I'm about to tell you, though we each came across the truth in different ways. In my case, and your grandpa's, it was our first next-door neighbor, Mr. Adams, who let the cat out of the bag. He was old when we were young, and had seen things in Europe during the First World War that drove him to drink. When he drank he often came over to talk with your grandpa. I didn't like it at first, but Mr. Adams was never violent or rude, just liked to talk, and one night I overheard him say, 'If you walk in Still Creek Wood enough times, you'll notice how none of the old trees were ever young, and none of the young trees ever grow old.'"

Grandma leaned forward. "He was right, you see. If you ever go up there again—though I'm not saying you should, even if you *are* older now—you'd see the same young saplings in the same places, same height, same branches, that were there when you were a child. There would be a few more, since Mrs. Forester had a still-born baby two years back and that sweet Schretengoss child died of leukemia, but besides them the saplings in the forest would be the same. And the older trees? The ones when I was young are the same as the day they appeared, but have since been joined by many, many others."

I shook my head. "What do you mean, 'appeared?'"

"Just like you saw all those years ago," Grandma said. "A tree that hadn't been there before, full-grown, pushed those old steps up so you could swing your legs from the lowest branch." She paused, allowing me to piece everything together so I could say it back to her, paraphrased and simplified, evidence of my understanding.

But I wasn't ready. Not yet.

"You mean…" I began.

"…that when someone in Still Creek has to leave, and that leave-taking involves a funeral home and last rites, Still Creek Wood gets a little larger," Grandma finished. "One tree larger, to be exact. Yes. You've got it."

I looked up the incline of the back yard, to where the tops of Still Creek Wood waved in a cool spring breeze.

"I believe it," I said at last, quietly.

Grandma took my hand. "Say it back to me."

"Whenever someone in Still Creek dies, Still Creek Wood gains a tree."

"Good."

Then we were silent, and it was the silence of deep thoughts.

Finally, "But why was I attacked? I did nothing wrong."

Grandma sighed. "Because some of those trees, like the people they used to be, are cantankerous. Some downright bad. Rotten. Your grandpa got along with most everyone in town, won the respect of all he knew. That's why he felt safe when he went walking in there, and why I didn't worry too much when you went along with him. But given half a chance, the bad will always work what mischief they can, and by yourself you weren't protected. Now maybe you can go back, if you have a mind. But if you do, promise me you'll be careful."

"But why would I want to go back?" I said.

"Oh heavens, did you forget the tree by the stone steps?"

"No, but…"

"Goodness, haven't you *guessed*?" Tears again came freely to my grandmother's eyes and spilled down her creased cheeks.

And I made the last, great connection.

Grandma must have seen the light in my face. "That's right," she said softly, and patted my hand. "That's right."

* * *

And now, age thirty, married and on the cusp of another era in my life, I wonder if I should finally go back. I didn't that day. Perhaps I was still too incredulous. Or too frightened. But now I want to go, I really do. Loss, that crushing wheel, has turned again.

I got the call this morning. Sometime during the night, Grandma passed away.

I keep wondering… will it be there if I go?

I'll choose a sunny day in early spring, the season when life in *all* its forms is granted renewal. I will walk up through the yard of the empty house, past the flower garden under the maple tree, the flagstone walk, and the tool shed; past the burn pile, the three overgrown pines, and the spring. I will enter the woods and find my way, with great care, to the old stone steps.

And will it be there? The second oak beside the first? New but not, full-grown and splendid?

Will the two trees rustle their leaves in the warm, still air, just for me?

The Saver

Their car broke down thirty miles from Bedford, the nearest town with a gas station. Mabel and Tony Palmer sat for a moment in the softly ticking Oldsmobile Cutlass, the rapidly warming air thick with mutual disbelief.

"Shit," said Tony, simply.

"There go our plans with Adam and Kathy."

He sighed, she sighed, and they both got out, slamming the doors shut behind them. Immediately the strong, cliff-side wind whipped at their hair, their clothes, bringing with it the salty tang of the sea and making them blink rapidly. On the driver's side a guardrail marked the edge of the road. Just beyond it the cliff descended, all sheer drop and red stone, for three hundred feet to meet the crashing waves.

"No reception," Tony muttered, sliding the useless phone back in his pocket. "This must be the last place in America that doesn't have it."

"There's a house up there," said Mabel, pointing to the top of the hill that rose steeply across the street. "We can ask for help."

"I hate asking help from strangers," said Tony.

"Then start pushing."

The seashell-paved driveway was winding and uneven. At the top, sweating and out of breath, they found themselves standing on a green, closely-manicured lawn. A small wooden windmill spun frantically in the wind. Glass and metal chimes clinked and rang from the porch of a small, neat cottage that seemed within inches of sliding down the hill, back end first, onto the road far below.

"It's quaint," said Mabel.

"In Big Sur, with a cliff-side view of the ocean, it's probably worth a million," said Tony.

"More than that," said a voice behind them.

Mabel let out a tiny yelp. They turned.

An old man of perhaps seventy was smiling at them beneath a frayed straw hat. The sleeves of his denim shirt were rolled up, his browned skin slick with sweat. He held a mud-encrusted shovel over one shoulder.

"Sorry," he added, and gave them a reassuring grin. "I was working yonder, in the field over the lip of the hill, and took the side path around when I saw you coming up."

The next thing he said was unexpected: "You need saved? They don't usually come up to the house if they need saved. Usually I got to go down to them."

Mabel and Tony cast a quick glance at each other and locked eyes. *A holy roller*, Tony thought. *Just great. Thick as flies everywhere.*

"Um, no, we don't need saved," Mabel said politely. "Our car broke down and we don't have cell phone reception. We need to call for a tow. That's all."

"Oh, hey, why didn't you say so?" The old man swung the shovel off his shoulder and impaled it with surprising force in the packed, shell-strewn drive. It stuck there, quivering, then stilled. "You can use my phone, and we can sit a bit on the back porch and have some lemonade while you wait for your tow. It'll take a little time. Name's Carl Budren. Pleased to meet you and come on in."

They followed him into the prim, tidy cottage. Dozens of seashells, stones, sea glass, and starfish, carefully glued into patterns, adorned the wood-stained walls in driftwood frames. The wicker furniture, worn but not dilapidated, was simple and inviting—a perfect fit. Mr. Budren dug a phonebook out of a drawer in his kitchenette, licked a calloused finger, found a page, found a number, and soon the local towing service was on its way.

Minutes later they found themselves sitting on the rickety, whitewashed porch overlooking a dizzying drop to the road, cliffs, and dark, crashing waves far below.

Mr. Burden joined them, a cold, sweating glass of lemonade in each hand.

"An hour 'til the truck comes, huh? Well, it's nice to have some company, even if you don't need saved." He sat down in a spare chair, sighing as his knee joints popped.

"No, sir," said Mabel. "We aren't the religious type. I'm afraid converting us is a battle you just won't win, if you'll excuse me saying so."

The old man's eyebrows narrowed, then he smiled and chuckled. The sound was faint, like a distant motor. "No, no, ma'am, you misunderstand me." He nodded down toward the cliffside road, where their car sat like a squat, injured beetle. "You don't know this spot, I take it. Just a random place your vehicle happened to break down."

"That's right," said Tony, bemused.

The old man reached into his pocket and pulled out a battered pack of cigarettes. "You mind?"

"No," said Tony and Mabel in unison, though both did.

Mr. Budren lit up. "Across the highway by the cliff, and about twenty feet further down the road from your car, there's a little jut of rock. An outcropping, like. On the other side of the guardrails. See it?"

They looked. They saw.

"For about forty years now, that's been known as End Point. Don't know why, but there's been more suicides there over the years than anywhere along this coast for two hundred miles in either direction. Hell, you'd have to drive down to Frisco's bridge to find a hotter spot."

They both looked again, longer this time.

"How many have jumped?" Tony asked, chewing a piece of ice from his lemonade.

Mr. Budren stroked his chin.

"In the last twenty years or so, I'd put the number somewhere around forty, maybe a few more. There was more before that, but I don't have the exact numbers."

Both Mabel and Tony started. Tony's mouth worked a little, but he said nothing.

"No one knows why?" Mabel finally asked.

"Well, I guess it's a couple things." Mr. Budren took a drag off his cigarette. The smoke plumed out his nostrils like the exhalation of a geriatric dragon. "First, it's a good view. Of course, there's plenty of those, but I guess that's something. I reckon the dying like a good view before they go. Second, all it takes is one or two jumpers before word gets out about a place. Then others copy the first. I don't know why, except maybe the desperate like being part of something, too. Something they can share with like-minded souls."

"Like a club," murmured Tony.

Mr. Budren nodded. "That's right, Mr. Palmer. An *exclusive* club."

He took another drag off his cigarette, and a far-away look palled his face. "An exclusive club," he repeated, voice little more than a murmur.

"Mr. Budren? What does that have to do with saving?"

Mr. Budren turned to Mabel, and in that quick moment his eyes focused again. "Ah! Yes, oh yes. Well, my daddy owned this cliff-side property for going on half a century but never did nothing with it. When he died I was about retirement age. I'd heard of End Point, so since I got the rights I thought I'd build a little house up here. Figured I could save some people if I spotted anyone who came by and looked ready to jump."

Mabel leaned forward. "That's the reason you moved here and built this house? To keep people from killing themselves?"

Mr. Budren nodded. "Yes, ma'am."

Tony shifted, his wicker chair creaking. "So how does it work?"

"Hmm?"

"Saving people."

Mr. Budren smiled widely. "It's real simple, mostly. I keep an eye out, you see. When I spot a car parked near End Point, or a motorbike, or whatever else, I head on down the drive to the road and see what's what. Usually someone'll be sitting in the car, or on the bike, or even standing on the point, sometimes on one side of the guard rail, sometimes on t'other. If I get there in time, that is. And if I do, I go on down and have a talk with them."

"You don't call the police?"

"No time for that, son. Not if they're settling in to jump. No. I just go down and have a talk with them. It's what works. It's what the moment needs."

Mabel took a small sip of lemonade. The ice clinked against her teeth. "But what do you *say*? I couldn't imagine being put in a situation like that, with a life on the line and everything riding on what words you choose."

Mr. Budren grunted. "Well, miss, you do have a point. It's a mighty tight spot, sometimes. But I knew it would be when I moved here. And that stress is worth it, when you save someone. To know they're *safe*. That's the payoff.

"But as to what I say…" He paused, thinking. "It depends, but usually I ask them what their favorite thing to do is in all the world. I keep 'em talking, have them tell me all about it. Everyone has something they love to do. So if I'm lucky they start talking, and I listen, and prod, and ask more questions, and finally I get around to saying, 'Now don't you want to do that again? Because you sure as hell can't if you're fish food in the Pacific.' Or something to that effect."

Tony raised his eyebrows. "That's it?"

Mabel jabbed him in the ribs, scowling. But Mr. Budren just smiled again. "One time it took five hours. Another, I made dinner for a woman and brought it out to her because she got hungry after talking so long. It was just the two of us sitting there, on the edge of that cliff, with Death circling round and round us. But she ate, and she came to, and she was saved."

He stubbed out his cigarette in a stained seashell ashtray and sat back in his creaking wicker chair.

"That's really something," Tony admitted.

"It really is, Mr. Budren," added Mabel. "That's incredible."

"Well," said the old man, sighing, "it soothes me, to do something. But I can't save 'em all. When I come down some mornings and find an empty car by End Point, I know I failed because I can't be there all the time. Then I call the police and they call a tow, and sometimes a body washes up down the coast, carried far on the current. Most often it's never found."

He brightened. "But it's worth all that. And I'm very content. Now, unless I'm mistaken, that's your tow truck! So I won't keep you any longer."

They looked. It was.

As they reached the front door, Mabel turned back and gave the old man a quick hug. "You're an amazing man, Mr. Budren. I'm glad we met you."

"Well thank you, darling," he replied, flashing a final warm smile.

Tony held out his hand. "Yeah, those are lucky people, Mr. Budren. The ones you saved. Glad we could meet."

The couple walked quickly down the hillside drive, Mr. Budren watching from the top. Faintly, he could hear Tony hailing the tow truck driver. He watched them for another ten minutes until the car was latched to the truck, and both truck and car were nothing more than glints of reflected sun, far away and receding, on the winding, cliff-side road.

Then he turned, retrieved his shovel, and walked purposefully across the well-tended yard and over the crest of a small rise. Beyond, a long, sunken field of scrub grass stretched away into the distance, just out of sight of the house.

"Lucky people," he repeated.

He picked his way carefully down the other side of the rise and stopped beside a half-filled pit. Next to it was a small mound of dirt. Whistling tunelessly, he smiled as he resumed shoveling—the young couple's interruption already all but forgotten.

A pale, thin hand stuck up from the pit like a wilted, diseased plant. Moments later, dirt covered it.

"Lucky people," he said a final time. He stopped to rest, wiping his brow and looking out at the dozens and dozens of faint, rectangular depressions in the earth that even the tall grass could not completely obscure.

"I sure did save them."

MATTIE

Shells

My cove is rimmed on all sides by high, steep outcroppings of sharp rock. Only one gravel road leads through them down to the beach. The beach is white sand and small pebbles. And shells, of course. Lots and lots of shells.

I've collected shells as long as I can remember, ever since I was a very little girl. I've always loved them. First, when we stayed at the cabin every summer, I collected everything I could find, but after my family moved here for good, I became more selective. Otherwise, where would I keep them all?

* * *

There are some wonderful rare kinds in the cove. You can find the best ones in late spring, in tide pools by the black rocks that jut out from the sand. And after a storm. Even in winter there are good shells to be found after a storm.

I get lonely real easy, now that we're at the cove all year round. There aren't many children nearby. But one evening in late-November, I looked up from my shell hunt to see a boy walking toward me from the opposite end of the beach.

He was tall and lanky, about twelve. A little younger than me. And he kept his head down. I knew what that meant. He was hunting shells, too.

I met him down by the rocks near the tide pools. Boy, was he surprised! He looked me over, real shy, and said, "I didn't know anyone else lived here."

"Me neither," I said. "Isn't it a little late in the year for a vacation?"

He shook his head. "My grandpa had a house on the other side of the cliffs. He died last month and my folks and my uncles have to go through everything and decide who gets what."

He paused. "They fight a lot, so I got out of there. I can't take it."

I felt bad for him and nodded in what I hoped was an understanding way. "What's your name?"

"Sam Gerts. What's yours?"

"Mattie. Hey, you like shells?"

Sam nodded. "Every beach I go to I look. But I don't see any good ones here."

"No, not this time of year. Not unless there's a storm, and then there's some great ones, really! But let's check over there."

I led him to a little tide pool basin separated from the dark ocean by just a foot or two of jagged stone.

"They collect here at high tide. Even in fall and winter you can come across nice ones if you're lucky."

We scanned the pool, its rocky bottom covered with shifting sand. Tiny, black fiddler crabs scuttled in dark corners. A hermit crab climbed among the mussels.

"There!" I said, as the current shifted the sand and revealed something white, pink, and sharp. "Grab it!"

Sam leaned forward and gave a yank. "It's heavy! I can hardly budge it!"

"Give it a *big* tug. A real hard pull."

He did, grunting, and the huge whelk sucked out of the sand.

"Hey! Hey, look at that!" he cried, beaming at the beautiful shell. It was a full foot long, its spiral perfect, the inside a smooth, polished pink.

He handed it to me. "You keep it. You saw it first."

"You grabbed it, it's yours."

"Thanks. That's really nice." He looked it over again. A big, goofy grin spread across his face. "It's the best one I ever got."

Then his watch beeped. "Oh, shoot. Dinner. I gotta get back." His face fell. "I don't want to, but I'll get in trouble if I don't. Mom's been real stressed through all this mess. Can't say as I blame her." He clambered down the rocks and back onto the sandy beach.

I felt real bad. I'd just made a new friend and now he had to go home.

"How long you staying at the cove?" I called out. He was already walking away.

Sam turned. "A week. Maybe a little longer. 'Til after Thanksgiving, at least. We just got in today. Hey," he took a few steps back, "you wanna meet again tomorrow? Same place?"

"Early in the morning or in the evening as the sun begins to set. That's when I come down."

"I'll be there."

My heart swelled.

* * *

The next week was terrific. We met every day, usually in the morning and evening, and spent the time walking, skipping stones in the surf (trying to make them go through as many wave crests as possible), and poking around in the hills.

And collecting shells.

I asked Sam about where he lived and he said far inland, in Arizona, and that he didn't really like his school. And I told him all about my family and the town we used to live in before we moved here full-time. But he never invited me to meet his parents, and I never invited him to meet mine. We were both shy, and besides, for Sam our time was a chance to escape all the family problems and sadness he had to deal with.

The cove was a place where we both felt comfortable and easy. And we found some great shells, too! Over a few days we gathered up a couple dozen good cowries, some beautiful, purple-streaked scallops, and even a conch the size of my fist. Sam found some shark's teeth, which really thrilled him, and I snagged a handful of ray egg pods, which I took home to dry.

At one point during those long days, Sam turned to me and said, "I think fighting is the dumbest thing ever. People say and do things they regret and can't ever take back. Take my Uncle Brock. He used to be nice. But he wants some paintings that belonged to my grandfather because he wants to sell them. Mom and Uncle Alex want to keep them in the family. Uncle Brock said they were selfish and always ganged up on him, and then Dad said something, then Mom, then Uncle Alex, and all back and forth until they were screaming and stamping and threatening, and now they're not talking anymore. I don't think I'll ever see Uncle Brock again."

Sam had never told anyone that, except me. He trusted me. That meant so much, even though I'd only known him a little while. And I understood how he felt.

* * *

The storm struck just two days before Sam had to leave. I should have been glad, but this one hit at a bad time. Sam and I were still out on the beach, skipping stones. The clouds got dark, but we just thought twilight was falling. Then, finally, Sam looked around and whistled. "We better get inside."

"Oh, we'll be fine," I replied.

And then the storm hit.

It was a real bruiser: a cold, hard shower with black, pressing clouds. The whole cove was covered in gloom and shifting light from blue, scattered lightning. Strong, gray waves lashed the shore. A bitter, spray-flecked wind drove us toward the water, but we fought our way back.

Sam shivered, raising his voice to be heard over the thunder. "Is your place close?"

No, I thought. *Don't tell. Not yet.*

"You go ahead home, Sam!" I yelled back. "I'll meet you tomorrow. I'll be fine!"

"No, I live too far away!" The rain had plastered his hair against his head and his chattering lips were pale. "Is your house nearby?"

I thought a moment. I was shy about my home. But I knew Sam trusted me. The things he'd told me all said so.

"Fine," I said after a long pause. "Follow me! We'll ride it out and you can head home later."

I led him along the beach, farther than I'd gone before with him, then up a thin path into the hills that ringed it. The rain was really hammering down now. Lightning flashed and thunder rolled across the sky.

"Almost there!" I called back to Sam.

We reached the cave: a small, black hole in the side of the hill—all by itself, hard to find, invisible from the shore.

"What's that?" Sam asked.

I shook my head and pulled him in after me.

It was very dark inside, but the falling day and the lightning provided some light. I shook out my hair and Sam ran a hand through his.

"Where are we, Mattie?" he asked, still breathing hard, water dripping off his nose. "This is a *cave*."

"It's OK," I said softly. "Come on."

I led him farther in. He followed slowly, hesitantly, and soon I heard his shoes crunch.

"Careful!"

"What is it?" he asked. "I can't see."

"Why, it's my shell collection, dummy! You're stepping on it!"

He stopped walking. I could barely see his face. "What is this place? Why are we here?"

"It's my home," I said. And before he could speak, I stepped forward and lit a candle. "Here, now you can see all my shells!"

I looked around the long, low space and smiled. It was cold but dry, and for ten feet back into the cave the floor was covered with shells. My shells. My whole collection. Every kind you could imagine. All shapes and sizes. Most of them perfect. They lay two feet deep in some places, piled almost to the ceiling in others.

"Your… your collection is *here*? Home? Mattie, I don't understand. I—"

He stopped.

"What's that smell?" he demanded in a hollow voice.

I winced. "Nothing. I mean… Sam, we're all here, you see. I would have told you before you left, but the storm kind of rushed things. Still, you trusted me. I know I can trust you, too."

"Mattie…" Sam's face was very pale. "In the corner, way back there… what *is* that?"

I followed his gaze. In the shifting candlelight, in the flashes of lightning, I could make out two dark shapes I knew very well.

"Give me the candle." Sam yanked it from my hand.

"Wait, Sam, I just—" I tried to hold him back but couldn't.

He thrashed through my shells, not bothering to be careful, until he stood over the slumped forms. He stared at them for a long, long time.

"Sam?" I said softly. "They're my parents, Sam. Or used to be. I was so worried what you'd think, I couldn't tell you…"

Suddenly, almost casually, he turned and threw up. He breathed hard, fast, and wiped his mouth. He stumbled away from the half-rotted bodies and moaned.

"It was my father, Sam," I told him quietly. "He had a bad time. He'd lost his job. One night he and Mom got to fighting. You know how it is. Anyway, he wasn't thinking straight. He took us up here, and that's when I saw the gun. He shot her, Sam. Then he shot himself."

"No," he wheezed, eyes wide. He stepped back from me slowly, like a sleepwalker, and tripped over something else.

Sam fell.

Don't look down, I thought.

He did.

"Dad shot me, too. Right after Mom."

And then Sam bolted upright, screaming and screaming, his face a white mask of shock. He stumbled past me, crunching shells as he passed. He sobbed, pulled in a harsh breath, screamed again, and ran.

"No!" I said, starting to cry. "Come back! That's not me, Sam! Not any more! It's just a shell! Just an empty shell!"

But he was already gone, his shrieks lost in the howl of the wind, and once again I was alone with my collection.

Wood Smoke

"My grandfather tilled this farm," Benjamin Collins told Blake Riggs, his grandson. "It ain't proper and it ain't right."

"You should buy one of those townhouses they want to build on it. You could, with the amount they're offering." Blake was 26, ambitious, with a master's degree in business management from Penn State. He lived in Pittsburgh, fifty miles away.

Collins looked at him with bemused impatience.

"Offering? *Demanding*, you mean. And to share all this with a hundred townies, talking into earphones like crazy people, power-walking, with manicured lawns and little, red foreign cars and rat-terrier dogs? No. I won't do it. *Can't* do it."

"*Have* to, Grandpa."

Collins sighed. "Come outside, kid."

With a hidden smirk, Blake followed him through the kitchen to the back porch. The view of the property was almost complete from this vantage—fallow ground, long untilled, and a great expanse of woodland. Maples, oaks, birches, and spruce pines sighed in a mid-summer breeze.

"See, Grandpa?" said Blake. "What do you need all this for, anyway? It hasn't been an active, productive farm in twenty-five years, and even then it didn't bring in much money."

"Money," Collins echoed.

"Right. And besides, look at all those trees! You're the proud owner of a half-assed scrub forest. To sell is the best option. But, hey, it isn't even an option now, is it? Not the way the town council raised your taxes."

"When I was a boy," Collins said quietly, not looking at his grandson, "my daddy used to thin the forest. Lots of trees die in a year, and of course saplings start to grow in the fields. Every autumn, close to Halloween, he and my uncles and my older brothers and me would cut them down and stack them all in great piles and set them on fire. Always around apple-harvest time. The *smell…*" He closed his eyes. "You know the smell of wood smoke, Blake?"

"I guess," Blake replied absently. "I don't know."

"There's nothing like it. If you did, you'd not forget. My daddy, he used to smoke cherry tobacco from his corncob pipe while he worked. Always did when he was outside, and farmers are *always* outside. And on those days when they lit the fires and Mother made hot apple cider and baked pumpkin pies, and all the neighbors came over, I remember sitting here on the back porch, smelling his tobacco and the wood smoke mixing together, and it felt like everything would always be all right and nothing would ever change."

"That's sweet, Grandpa, but things *do* change."

The faraway look in Collins' eyes faded. "Anyway, I'll sell, but they're letting me keep the old house; that's the condition if I stop fighting. Isn't that nice? A stand-up thing to do. Change… yeah, things change. Some things. So it goes." He passed a hand across his brow, wiping off a sheen of perspiration. "And I'm getting tired, so I think I'll head upstairs and let you head home. Thanks for coming out and visiting your old ancestor."

He led Blake to the front door.

* * *

An hour later and three blocks away, the steamed windows of Maggie's Eat n' Smile Diner hid the two men in the front booth from the view of anyone walking down Main Street.

"Does he know?"

Blake snorted. "How can he? Anyway, he's keeping the house, so we'll have to work around that, but I don't think he'll be any more trouble. Not like before, when he went up against the council with that damned petition. He'll sell. He told me. He can't afford the tax increase. That's got him."

Max Nelson, President of the Still Creek Town Council, beamed. "That works out for all of us, then."

"He got quite a piece of change from the deal. I'd rather inherit that when the time comes than a useless bit of wilderness."

"Well, hell, kid, you're overlooking the best part!"

"What? That my company's doing the developing?"

They both laughed.

"Here's to a mean, ornery son-of-a-bitch."

"Which one? Him or me?"

Glasses clinked. Steaming dinners arrived.

* * *

"I haven't seen you for upwards of a year." Collins, a little older, a little slower, appraised his grandson with shrewd but tired eyes.

"Sorry, Grandpa. I've been snowed under, that's all. Lots of work."

"I figured. Busy man. Plenty to keep up with out there in the city. Thanks for coming."

Blake nodded. "It was nice you invited me. How's the view from the back porch now?"

"Come see."

They stepped through the kitchen door into the crisp autumn air that filtered through the screens.

"There's your view," Collins murmured dryly.

The old fields and forest were gone, cut down, bulldozed over. All that remained was a muddy, flat expanse from which the wooden shells of four-dozen townhouses rose like matchstick models in perfect rows.

"Wow, they're really making progress!" Blake exclaimed, absently rubbing his hands together. "Amazing."

"Yes, ain't it though?"

"See? Everything changes, Grandpa. Just like I said. Everything changes, and it isn't so bad."

His grandfather clapped him on the back. "Well, you might be right, kiddo. But I gotta be honest. One thing doesn't change. Not ever."

"Hmm? What?"

"I'm still a mean, ornery son-of-a-bitch. Always will be."

Blake blinked, then laughed nervously. "Well, I kind of like you anyway."

"Why *thank* you, kiddo." Collins gave him another good-natured pat and pulled a corncob pipe from his back pocket. He sighed, packing it carefully with tobacco from a bag he produced from his shirt.

"I didn't know you smoked, Grandpa."

"This is the very first time since I was a young man. Bought the pipe and tobacco down at Stockton's just this morning."

"What's the occasion?"

Collins patted his pockets. "Where'd I leave my matches? Oh, here we go." He pulled a box from another pocket, struck a wooden match with his thumbnail, lit the pipe, and inhaled deeply.

The smell of burning cherries filled the air.

"That takes me back," he said through clenched teeth. "Smells are powerful when it comes to bringing back memories. You have any special smells that bring back memories, kiddo?"

Blake shook his head. "Nope. Can't say that I do, Grandpa."

"That's a hell of a shame. You know," Collins added abruptly, "Mrs. Gerts down the street is an old friend."

"Is that so?"

"Yep. I've known Myra Gerts for fifty years if a day. Small town, you know. And she tells the best damn stories. She hears things, you see, from here and there around town. Especially when she takes her supper at Maggie's Diner."

"Oh?" Blake looked distracted. He was squinting hard toward the distant townhouse frames.

"Oh, yeah. And one of those stories—one of her favorites, in fact—is about an uppity young man from Pittsburgh who talks too loud and...Hey, but you look distracted, Blake. Why? It's a nice autumn day. Falling leaves, cherry tobacco...there's just one thing missing."

Blake blinked, took a step forward, stopped, eyes fixed on a spot in the distance. "Is that... is that *smoke?*"

"Hmmm?"

"*Smoke.* It... it is! Oh God! It's... *they're all—*"

"Well, would you look at that!" Collins opened the screen door and stepped out onto his back walk. Blake followed, mouth opening and closing like a shocked fish in cold air.

In the distance, flames licked higher as pine boards burned.

"Grandpa! Grandpa, call the fire de—"

The old man smiled. "*That's* what was missing, kiddo. Damn, but that's what it was."

"What? *What?*"

"That other smell," Collins said, removing the pipe from his mouth. "You can't have one without the other. It just wouldn't do."

"*Other* smell?" Blake had turned a deathly shade of pale.

"Wood smoke," Collins said, breathing deeply. "Don't you just love it? When I smell that and cherry tobacco mingling in the cool autumn air, it's like everything will always be all right and nothing will ever change. Oh, but I guess I told you that before. Here now, breathe deep. You'll *never* forget this day."

Blake ran around the house and into the street, screaming for help.

Collins shook his head, clamping the pipe between his teeth again. Cold, he stuffed his hands in his pockets. One of them found and shook the box of matches.

Half empty, it sounded like a rattlesnake.

The Return

Isabelle Benson lay under white sheets in the thin bed in the calm room and waited for someone to arrive. Someone always did. She never had to wait long. Everyone was very attentive. Everyone asked about her and how she was feeling. Today she thought she felt fine.

Some time later that felt like a little while but might have been longer, the door to her room opened inward. A figure entered. She had expected the door to open because someone always entered, but *this* visitor, this *man*…

She gasped, and in her thin wrist her pulse fluttered like a dove.

The man was middle-aged, dark-haired, chisel-chinned, kind-faced and tall. He wore a light spring sports coat that fit his good frame like a latex glove—every contour and angle cut to match what the cloth covered.

"You," Isabelle whispered. Then, as if reassured by her own voice, she said it again, louder.

The man said something in reply, something she didn't hear, so she continued, "It's been… oh, God, it's been so *long*. You look fine. You always did. Come and sit down by the bed. It's a comfy chair. Someone bought it for me."

The man did as she asked. He smiled and placed his hand on her arm, squeezing gently.

"Burton," she said firmly, and with the word out in the air, in the world, something clicked, a dam broke.

"You came back. They said you never would, but you did. Oh, sweet Jesus, you came *back!* How have you been? *Where* have you been? There's so much I have to tell you. The children, what they're doing and what they've done. And Mama and Papa. They…They…"

He said something. It was too soft, she couldn't hear, but the expression on his face conveyed all.

"I know," Isabelle continued. "It was hard. Very hard. I think about them all the time. Mama went first some years back. Died while talking with Martha in the kitchen. Martha asked her a question and she didn't answer, and that was that. And Papa? He passed during a snowstorm. Crashed his truck trying to get home from the mill. And there's been others, Burton. Lots of others. Oh, you've been gone so *long*. They said you were gone for good..."

She paused, breath rasping in her lungs.

"And I believed them," she finished.

Again he said something, paused, then said something else. Still, his voice was too low, too faint.

"You murmur now," she said. "Always was a quiet one. Either you didn't talk or you talked soft. But don't worry." She scanned his face. "I can read you fine."

Isabelle stared at the familiar features for a long moment. The face seemed frustrated, confused, so she pulled it close and touched the smooth cheek. When she removed her palm he was calm again. Resolved like always. There was steel in him. She had always loved that.

"There now," she said. "And speak up so I can hear you."

"I said I've missed you, too," he said, voice slow and clear.

This time she heard him.

"There was so much to say that I never said," she said. "Things ended badly. It was my fault. I know it now, and I knew it then, but I couldn't do nothing about it because you left me." Rare tears filled her eyes. She wiped them away without thinking. "Burton, I always thought you wasn't ever coming back. I knew it like I know my own face. I was *certain*."

"I'm here now," he said. "I came back. For a little while."

"A *little* while?"

He nodded.

"But I don't want you to go away again."

"It's not up to me."

"What?"

He repeated himself.

Isabelle paused, considering. "I guess I won't question it. You're here now, and that's something. And here, now, there's something I've got to tell you."

He leaned forward, nodding his head.

She swallowed. Her mouth was dry. Her hand trembled as it touched the familiar head of dark hair. "Before you left, we fought. You remember. You couldn't possibly forget."

Again, he nodded.

"It wasn't about anything in particular. Something about the garden. You wanted tulips and I wanted white lilies. That night, when you left, the last thing I said was that you weren't good enough for me. That I should have looked ahead before we married and thought better of it. That you were a fool. And then… later that night… in the morning, you…"

He shook his head and touched a finger to his lips. Isabelle's agitation diminished.

"I wanted to say I'm sorry, Burton," she said. "All these years, these long years, and you were gone and I couldn't say it. Not so it counted. But now I can. Please. Oh, God, please forgive me."

A pause. Then, very clearly, he said, "I forgave you long ago. Remember that. Never forget it."

Isabelle sighed, old air rushing from her lungs like stale autumn wind.

And then she slept.

* * *

"How was Grandma?"

Eric Benson poured himself a glass of lemonade and sat down across the kitchen table from his mother.

"Fine," he said, "but her hearing aids weren't working well. Hey, Mom?"

"Hmm?"

"How did Grandpa die? I know you were young."

The surprise showed on his mother's face. "Was Grandma talking about Daddy? She hardly ever mentions him. Keeps her grief buried deep."

Eric nodded.

"I was seven," his mother said. "They had a fight, and Daddy was upset and went to bed early. And he never woke up. Massive heart attack. He was only forty-one years old. Just five years older than you. God, that was over fifty years ago."

She looked up. "What did Grandma say about him?"

Eric took a big swallow of lemonade. "Nothing. She just said she'd been thinking about him."

A long silence.

"How was she?" his mother said finally. "Mentally, I mean? The staff at The Pines seem to think she's getting worse. Was it a good day or a bad day?"

Eric opened his mouth to speak, then paused, considering.

"A good day," he said at last. "It was a very good day."

The Subject

Halloween. Yeah, it's Halloween, imagine that! But if you look at it, that makes everything fit. Of course I don't know for sure. I mean, I wasn't around when it happened. But if it's not true, none of it makes any sense. So it's gotta be true, unless you can come up with something better. Yeah. Yeah, I'll tell you what I know. Then we'll see if you think what I think.

When I was a kid, Halloween was that perfect holiday. I mean, we got all dressed up, pretended to be what we weren't, flexed our imaginations. Monsters and myths and television characters. Yeah, we *pretended.* And I guess when you look at it, we were facing our fears, too. Don't you think? And the thing we fear worst of all is Death, isn't it? Sure it is. We fear what we don't understand, and that tops the list. And Halloween, it's a night for facing Death head-on, right? Staring it down and saying, "You don't scare me." And sure it did, but somehow Halloween made it all a bit easier. But that's not all there is to it. I know that now. After today, I know it. Halloween goes a lot deeper than that.

Where should I start? What he was like? OK. And how I knew him? And then what happened? I can do that.

Saul. He was a good guy. The best way to describe him was intelligent but easy-going, without that fake blasé attitude that usually comes to mind when you think of graduate-level arts majors. I mean, he wouldn't distance himself from those around him, and more than that, he usually went out of his way to be friendly. But when he painted, he unplugged the phone, locked himself in his house, and laid low for a few hours, sometimes six or seven at a stretch. He loved doing what he did. He never showed me anything he was doing until it was done, but that makes sense. I'm the same way with my graphics, and—

Yeah, I'm a grad student too. Study 3-D animation, same year as Saul. Nope, no classes together. We met as undergrads four years ago and continued on here 'cause the university has good programs in our subjects. So we've known each other a long time. *Knew.* We understood each other. Been good friends all along. Amazing. I mean—

What? Okay. Fine, I'll stick to it. In August, at the beginning of the semester, Saul began painting live models in his classes—some nudes, others clothed, and that really kept him on his toes, since I guess he hadn't worked in that area much before. He really enjoyed it, I could tell. Whenever I came over he was in his room with the door shut, sketching out hands, feet, necks, muscles. He told me once, maybe last month I guess it was, he said, "I'm capturing emotion like I never could with fruit." That really cracked me up, but I saw what he was getting at. I think he felt he'd found a new niche.

I didn't get to see him as much as I'd have liked, since we both had our classes and our studies and our side-jobs, and I had my girlfriend. That was a sore spot for Saul, the whole relationship thing. Why? Oh, that's kind of a long—well, 'cause we knew each other for over four years, and all during that whole time I was dating Suzie, but Saul, he couldn't find anyone who suited him. He must've gone through a good dozen relationships, not to mention one-night stands, most with women, even some with men. He said he tried homosexuality "just to see what it was like." That's Saul. Always trying something new. He'd do anything twice.

Anyway, around our senior year as undergrads, Saul started turning sour about what he called "the whole *love* thing." I mean, if I even brought *up* Suzie, that's all it took to set him off. And remember, Saul was usually easy-going...He was obviously having trouble, I guess because so many of his friends seemed happy with their partners and he was alone. He didn't believe in love, or claimed not to. Said not everyone was lucky enough to find a match suitable for both partners, or something like that. He always asked, "How do you know Suzie is the right girl?" or said, "Don't move too fast into marriage. You never know." It used to piss me off. And man, when he found out Suzie and I were *engaged*? You should have seen him. Speechless. Red-faced. I'd never seen him like that before, and never did again. Eventually he got over it, mainly because we'd been friends for so long, and I think because he realized one man's discontent isn't necessarily every man's, but it took a good while to smooth things over. He's passionate, and when he gets convinced he's right, it takes him a while to compromise, let alone admit that maybe not everyone sees things the same. Easy-going but a bit bull-headed. Yeah, that's Saul.

Was Saul. God. I mean, *was*.

Anyway, that's why I was so surprised when he came into The Easy on Thursday three weeks ago (that's when we always met for drinks, since it was almost the weekend and neither of us work on Thursdays) and, man, he *smiled* when conversation turned toward relationships and I brought up Suzie. What date exactly? Well… I guess it was October 12th. Yeah, since today is Halloween. Yeah, yeah I'm sure. October 12th.

So when he came in, it was almost like he was looking for an excuse to start talking, like he'd been waiting to say something but hadn't wanted to speak out of the blue. That's Saul for you. *Was*.

"Hey, guess what? I met someone last week," he said, and damn but his eyes didn't light up when he said it. That was strange. I hadn't seen him excited about a girl, or about *anyone*, for that matter, in over a year. Sure, he got laid sometimes, he didn't go without that, but to talk about it, and to talk about it like he was happy about it, that was something else.

Anyway, I asked him about this new girl of his, kind of amazed and all, and taking it slow and careful in case this turned out to be the start of one of those sarcastic rants of his, but he was for real. Very earnest, very serious. He said he'd met her the previous Saturday. Said she came to his door looking for someone else, got the wrong house or something, and 'cause it was raining outside he thought he'd at least invite her in since she looked cold and kinda wet. I mean, he was a considerate guy, and you know where his house is, all the way out in the country where the rent's cheap. It's pretty far off from any other place.

I guess she declined, said she'd drive on, but then the rain picked up. You remember how it was that night? Flooding all over the place, washed-out roads, and you couldn't see five feet in front of your face to drive. It lasted almost two hours before it began to calm down. So she stayed, and she and Saul got to talking.

Yeah, of course he told me her name. I already told you he said it was Lucy. Sorry that doesn't help much, but he never mentioned a last name. And that's another thing that should've bugged me. I'm not sure if even *he* ever found out what it was. In fact, I'd bet he didn't, considering. What did she look like? "Willowy," Saul told me. And long blonde hair. About our age.

No, I never met her. Not once. I always figured I would, you know. I always figured there would be plenty of times when we'd all go out together, me and Suzie and Saul and her. But now… now, just the *thought…*

Gimme a minute, would you? Thanks. Just a minute.

Yeah. Yeah, I'm OK now. So they were talking, and then Saul said she started looking at some of his canvases, going from one to the next very slowly, very carefully examining each one. He kept the finished ones on the walls in the living room. They made him feel comfortable. Maybe it sounds vain, but I can understand why he did it. I'm the same way. Art's an expression of your feelings, your desires, what's important to you. It's an expression of yourself. Anytime I finish a rendering I'm proud of, up it goes.

He said she was really smitten with them, really smitten. That never did much for him, being complimented, since it was easy to be polite and easier to be insincere. That was one of his favorite phrases. But he said she seemed to know something about art, or about oil painting at least, and that her compliments were worded in technical terms. She even criticized a little, which *really* impressed Saul. And so they fell into some deep conversation—the kind of talk he couldn't get with almost anyone else. I could tell it excited him, having someone to talk to like that, someone who could keep up with his thoughts and theories and views, then insert her own and make him think. And finally, after three or four hours, he asked her to come back for lunch on Monday afternoon.

Yes, that would have been October 9th. I'd just bought pumpkins and decorated the apartment. I love Halloween. *Used* to. Not anymore. Not after today.

And so she did meet up with him again. She came back for lunch. And man, according to Saul, sparks *flew!* He said nothing physical took place, but when she left his house early that evening she'd already agreed to model for him, to be his subject for a series of paintings he was about to begin for his 538 class. Finding a good subject is tough, unless you want to use the people the class provides, and those aren't usually best. So that was good for him.

But Saul wasn't just happy, he was *thrilled.* She had a good mind *and* she was beautiful. I mean, it was as if after so long, after such a drawn-out period of building up a wall against a serious relationship, he was finally daring to peek over it and have a look around. He was attracted to her, and on more than one level. She meant something to him… connected with him. He was *interested* in Lucy. He *wanted* to know her better. She was good for him, that's the best way I can put it. Or I thought she was. I don't know, but there must've been something about her he'd been hoping to find for a long, long time—

Oh, God… oh, God…

Yes, thanks. Just… just… yeah, that's better. A cigarette beats caffeine any day. Calms the nerves when coffee riles them up.

So Saul was happy that night in The Easy, and we drank for a few hours, and talked about lots of things, but mainly about relationships. Saul also mentioned he'd met with Lucy at his house the day before—yes, the 11th—and started his sketches. He said she had no qualms about posing nude for him, no modesty. It was all for the sake of art, or so he claimed she said, although I bet he was hoping it was more than that. I could tell he thought it was.

And he said she had an absolutely beautiful body. "Stunning," he said. "Close to perfect."

I didn't hear from him again until the following Thursday—yeah, the 19th—when we met again, same time, same place, for our weekly thing. I'd had a rough few days, since classes were pressing with their deadlines, and my advisor was being a bear about my latest series of revisions. I didn't feel like talking much, or if I did, I wanted to talk about how much everything sucked. You know, to get it off my chest. That's what Saul and I usually talked about. Stuff like that. But Saul, he wanted to talk about Lucy instead.

He said he'd finished five oil paintings in four days. That he hadn't had more than four hours' sleep a night in the past week but felt great. Five paintings in four days? Man, that's output, especially on top of classes and everything else. And he said they were big canvases! That they were still drying but would set soon. He also claimed to be churning out charcoal sketches, and that Lucy never seemed to get tired of posing. That she was the perfect subject. Then he went on about all the great conversations they had, and how much they had in common, although he never mentioned what her major was, or even if she was in college. It was kind of funny, because, you know, I'd ask questions about her, and he said he didn't know the answers, as if that was completely natural. He said he didn't care.

Man, he even said he cooked for her, which I can hardly imagine, since Saul couldn't boil water without burning it. He went on about how close they were getting, and how he was hoping their relationship would turn into something bigger. Something even closer. He nudged me when he said that. God.

So I ended up listening to him instead of complaining about my week, and drinking more 'cause I wasn't doing most of the talking. I called it an early night, I guess since I was in kind of a bad mood and wasn't finding room to vent. Saul said he'd call me the following week about getting together again on Halloween. Yeah, today. I would have been with him at The Easy right now, at the costume party they have every year.

Saul called on Monday night. He said he'd finished another oil and was coming down the home stretch on plans for a few more. It was amazing. Those paintings can take *weeks*, especially the way Saul had always worked. He was still in a fine mood, although he sounded tired. Even so, since I was a bit perkier we chatted for a long time. He actually let me do most of the talking, so I went on and on about my workload, my Master's project, and stuff like that. We only touched on Lucy once, when he said she was coming over to see him again the next day, and he was going to try to "step up the pace with her," as he put it. I wished him luck. I truly hoped the relationship *would* move to the next level. He deserved some happiness, some contentment. And then we hung up. End of conversation.

Could I have another cigarette? Thanks. Sorry to bum, but I've really got a craving. Thought I was going to quit, but I guess not. Not for a while, anyway. I'll take the addiction for a bit longer. I think I'm going to need it.

Hmm? Last night. Do we have to talk about it right now? Can't I get something to eat? Fine, then. Yeah, I understand. It's just that it's been a bit of a… yeah.

Last night Saul called again, and this time, God, there was something wrong. I'd never heard him so upset.

"I pushed her away!" he said. "She's gone!"

"What happened?" I asked. "Why did she leave?"

Saul said, "I don't know, I put my arm around her, kissed her, and she kissed me back, was really getting into it, but then she just went cold—*so* cold—and she pulled away. I asked what I'd done, but she wouldn't talk about it. She just stood up, got her coat, and made for the damn door."

"She didn't say anything at all?" I asked. "No explanation?"

"She said she couldn't do it!" Saul said. "Said she didn't feel right about the whole thing and had to go. And that's all. That's all! I can't believe it. I didn't do anything wrong!"

"I'm sure that's true." And even if he had, I knew he sure hadn't meant to.

"No, no, I must have done *something*," he insisted. "I did something, and I drove her away, and now she might never come back. I couldn't handle that. I really couldn't."

And I said, "Well, maybe you could buy roses, stop by her house, see if you can talk it out together. Who knows what she's thinking? But if there's a connection, you need to go after her, to at least *try*. Sometimes there's something deeper at work—something in her past, some insecurity from way back. Like I said, you can't just assume it's something you did. And maybe if you put in the effort now, it'll show her things will be all right later on down the road; that she can feel comfortable with you, no matter what."

"But I *can't* go over to her house. Don't you get it? I just can't."

"Sure you can, Saul," I told him. "You just get up and go, and think about it later."

At that he just laughed. It was a desperate, flat, hopeless sound. And then he said, "But I don't know where she lives."

That brought me up short.

"You don't know where she *lives*?" I repeated.

"No, she never told me. She's shy, sometimes. Maybe she's poor. Ashamed of where she lives or what she does. That's the impression I always get. So I can't go find her… I can't."

Well, you've gotta admit, that's strange. Even then, I thought so. But I pushed all those thoughts away. Saul needed help.

He was devastated, crying with big, gulping sobs. Usually he was so calm about things that upset him, at least on the outside, but I guess Lucy really pushed his buttons the right way. She meant something to him. She was something special. Hearing him like that made me feel… well, you know. I hadn't heard him cry before, not even softly, but here he was, bawling his eyes out. It's hard to hear your friends in pain.

He calmed down after a while, though when I suggested he give her a call and talk about it, he said he didn't have her phone number. He didn't seem to think it was odd, but oh, man, isn't that the first thing you get when you want to see someone, even as a friend? And that's when I realized I knew virtually nothing about her. I wondered if he did, either—if he knew *anything about her at all*. But again, I didn't think much more about it until today.

So, after about an hour and a half, maybe around 10:30, we hung up. He'd promised me he was going to get some rest, take it easy, maybe watch a horror movie countdown on A&E. We were going to go over the whole thing again this evening at the bar and see if we couldn't find some way of fixing the damage. And then we planned on going to that Halloween party…

Could I have a break now? I really need a break. Thanks, ten minutes should do. Yeah, just to stretch. Water would be great. A Coke would be better. Sure, thanks.

I was asleep when Saul called back. No wonder. I mean, it was 3:30 in the morning. Today. Halloween. Oh, man, I'll never celebrate it again. No parties, no costumes, no candy, no movies...

Nothing. Not ever.

All I could hear was screaming. And distortion, because the screaming was so loud. I'd never heard anything like it. He sounded like a wild animal, like a dog howling and baying.

Finally he lowered his voice a little, but he kept repeating himself, over and over.

"She's *dead*," he said. "She's *dead*." He kept saying it, again and again: "She's *dead*, she's *dead*, she's *dead*..."

I talked to him. I don't know what I said, trying to get him to stop, and finally I ended up yelling at him to shut up, to just *shut up and tell me what happened*, but his voice raised with mine until we were both screaming at the top of our lungs, me telling him to shut up, and Saul just repeating, "She's *dead!* She's *dead!*" over and over. If I'd been there with him in person, I probably would have slapped him, like they do in the movies when someone's hysterical.

I need a glass of water. No, not another Coke, and definitely not coffee. Maybe another cigarette, too? God, look at my hands... thanks.

He quieted down after five or six minutes. Maybe a little more or less, I don't know. Either way, it was a pretty long time to be screaming that loud. By then we were both hoarse, and I was afraid he was going to hang up, that I'd hear the *click* of the phone. And that would have scared me, because he was so upset, and you never know what a person could do when they're that upset...

But he stayed on the line. I could hear him gasping.

"What happened?" I asked again, trying hard to keep calm.

"Lucy's dead," Saul responded, almost in a whisper.

"Okay, okay, now listen… are you *sure* she's dead? I mean, absolutely *certain*?"

"Yes!" he said. "Yes, I'm sure of it! I've never been so sure of—"

That tone was creeping back into his voice, and his voice was rising again, getting louder. So I cut him off.

"How did it happen?" I asked. I just wanted to get the facts out of him, you see? And to keep him calm. Man, how I kept *my* voice calm, I'll never guess. Maybe I didn't believe it was true. Like I was in shock or denial, you know? It all seemed so crazy.

"I don't know how it happened," Saul said. "I don't know, I don't know, I don't know…"

"But you know she's dead?" I demanded. "I don't understand."

Then Saul, he just exploded again. "Neither do I! Neither do I!" And then he started shrieking, and he didn't stop for an awful long time.

I kept quiet, let him wear himself out, and finally, after a good while, he did. And he didn't hang up, either, although at one point he dropped the phone. Once he was calm again I asked, "Where is she?"

"I don't know!" he wailed. "God, she could be anywhere. Anywhere! *I've got to get out of here.*" That's what he said: that he had to get out of there. And he should've. He should've just gotten out and run.

Again and again I told him to tell me where she was, or where he thought she was. I told him I had to know, he had to tell. That the only way to get to the bottom of things, to make things better, would be to tell me, and that we could take it from there, we could work it all out.

And over and over, he said he didn't know. That he didn't *want* to know. His exact words? "I don't know, and I don't ever want to find out. Hopefully far away." That's what he said: "Hopefully far away." I didn't understand it. None of it made any sense.

Then I heard a muffled thumping on his end of the line, like a knocking, and his breath, it hitched in his throat, and then he started breathing real hard, real fast, like he was hyperventilating or having some sort of attack. And finally I heard a sobbing noise. Yeah, it was him. I'm sure of it. And I heard that knocking again, much louder this time. Yeah, like knocking on a door. I asked what was going on, who it was at the door, but he just sobbed one final time, and paused, and said, "I gotta go," and that's when he finally hung up. I yelled into the phone, but nothing. He was gone. I called back, over and over, but he didn't answer. So after 15 minutes more I called you guys, then I jumped in the car and beat it over to his place as fast as I damn well could.

When I showed up, two cop cars were already there, and three of you guys in uniform were standing around by the door, so I got out and went up to meet them, and they told me to stand back. I remember one started to call out Saul's name, over and over, louder and louder. The door? Hell, you saw it—splintered apart and ripped half off its hinges, forced open and inward.

They went inside, and I heard someone say "Shit," and then another said, "Holy Mary." That's when I said the hell with it, I'm going to find out what's going on, I have to know, and I rushed in past them before they had a chance to stop me. Of course, they weren't even thinking about me. Their attention was elsewhere.

And then they brought me here, to answer your questions and tell you what I know. And now I'm done, and I'd really like to go home, if that's OK.

…If I have to, I will. But if you're gonna ask what I think you are, then… yeah, good, please make them quick. Sorry, but… just make them quick.

Saul was… he was dead, of course. I knew that right away. He looked—I—God, this can't be happening, you know? This just doesn't happen. This can't happen. And it's Halloween. The jack o' lanterns were still burning on his porch. There's *no way*. It's supposed to be a *fun* holiday. All about using the imagination, you know? Not real. But this *is* real. I can't deny what I saw. Saul looked… there was no color in his face, and his hair was white… *fucking white!* And his eyes were wide, and his mouth was open, and he was slumped down beside the coffee table, looking up, his head against the base of the couch.

And then one of the officers ran out of the house, and I could hear him retching on the porch, and the smell mingled with the smell of burnt pumpkins.

And that's when I looked up.

I'll never forget it, those paintings. They were on every wall, some huge, as big as this table, others more traditional size. I'm sure you'll see them soon if you haven't already. You haven't? Fine. Yeah, I'll tell you. I don't want to, but… they were all labeled clearly in the bottom right corners, each one, and each label read "Lucy Series," followed by a number.

Don't you see? All that time she'd fooled him. He'd seen what she'd wanted him to see, even as he was unconsciously painting her as she really looked. I know that now, and don't try and tell me any different. I won't buy it.

But Halloween… on Halloween, I guess she decided to come clean, so to speak. There's a power to the day, like in all the old stories. That must be it. And so today he finally saw what she was, and somehow, I can't imagine, got her out of the house, and called me.

But she came back.

The paintings. Yeah, I'm getting there. I'm ready…

They were portraits of a skeleton. In some it was covered in a sort of white dress, or cloak, but the fabric looked mildewed, like it'd been exposed to the elements for a long time. Some were full-body paintings, nothing covering the subject, and the skeleton, God help me, it wasn't a *clean* skeleton, if you know what I mean, and on its head was a thin crown of matted blond hair. One of the paintings was a detail of just the head and shoulders. And yeah, that's when I lost it, and I guess they had to haul me out of there. I started screaming and couldn't stop…

Yeah, I'm sure she's dead. But he didn't kill her. You didn't find a body, did you? And you won't, either. She's out there. Walking the evening streets right now, as she really is. Among all the costumes, who would ever notice? And tomorrow maybe she'll look different again, *alive* again, and some other poor soul will find her attractive.

Attractive.

I can't say anything else. I'll lose it. But it all makes sense, doesn't it? What was it Hamlet said? "There are more things in heaven and earth, Horatio, than are dreamt of in your philosophy." That says it all.

No, no more questions. Please. Please, don't ask any more. That's all I know, and tons more than I want to. No. No more. *Enough.*

Par One

"Oh, for God's sake!"

Livid, Charlie Neilson stared ahead, the smell of the Atlantic strong in his nose, his patient wife, Sarah, at his side.

Bethany Beach hummed around them: young parents led by restless children toward ice cream stands; bronzed teens loitering outside Beachfront Fries or strolling up the boardwalk, slick with suntan lotion, body boards attached to wrists with neon cord; and the elderly, a small but ever-present minority, quietly dining at outside cafés and sitting on boardwalk benches looking toward the horizon, thinking immutable thoughts.

Out of all these people, only Charlie stood stock-still, glaring intently and breathing hard, face a sunburned beet.

"Sarah," he said slowly.

"What, Charlie?"

"They tore the damn thing down and built a GAP over it!"

Sarah scrutinized the generic-looking chain store with mild disinterest. "What did they tear down?" she asked. "Which place? You've mentioned so many."

"The putt-putt golf course!" he replied, grinding his teeth. "It's been there fifty years, and sometime in the last few they tore it down, paved it over, and built *this* goddamned monstrosity. Hell, if they'd had room I bet they would have built a WalMart! It'd figure, it really would. And I guess this shouldn't surprise me, either."

Charlie and Sarah had been married two years. Charlie, a teacher, had saved up for this trip over six months, anxious to share his childhood vacation town with his new wife—to experience the old magic with someone new.

"What I wanted, what I really wanted, was to play that golf course with you," he said.

Sarah slid her hand into his. Without realizing, he gripped it hard and continued.

"An old man ran it. He owned half the town, did it for fun. Cost fifty cents to play, never more, no matter *what* year it was. And he had a little Scottie dog named Toto. There was a loop-the-loop, an old lighthouse with an eighty-watt bulb in the top, a rotating windmill, a mote bridge that rose and fell! And a metal ramp, a dozen sand traps, a stream you had to knock the ball over… and then, finally, Hole 18, a tiny bridge of wood with a hole at the end and a pit on either side. Get a Par One and you won a free game!"

"Did you ever win?" Sarah asked.

"Nope, never did. Mom, Dad, and me—we always missed, every single time. And when I was little I always figured next year would be the one, and then, that last year before high school when we moved too far away, I figured I'd come here again when I was older, married, maybe with children, and… but no." He shook his head. "Stupid of me to imagine, after all these years."

"Not stupid," said Sarah. "Sweet. But look around! This place is still full of life. Lots to do, lots to see, not too busy, not too lazy. We're going to have a great week."

"Hey," said Charlie, approaching a teenage clerk who had just emerged from the Gap for a cigarette. "Remember the old putt-putt golf course that used to be here? When did it close?"

The young man cupped a hand around his lighter and exhaled a plume of blue smoke. "Don't ask me," he said. "This is just my summer job. Live in Baltimore the rest of the year."

Sarah pulled at her husband's arm. "Dinner, Charlie. I'm hungry. There's a nice looking place around the corner. It's their Grand Opening Week. Bethany Bayou, it's called."

"No, no," said Charlie. "Suddenly I have a terrible headache. For me, a corndog and bed. Tomorrow will be better. You go out and have a good time."

* * *

The evening passed, the night passed, and in the early predawn morning Sarah, who *hadn't* had a good time the previous night, stole out of bed, left her husband snoring gently beneath sheets that smelled of sand and salt, and was back before he woke up.

After shutting the door with a slam, she shook Charlie's mattress, pinched his cheek, blew in his ear, and tugged his hair until he grumbled and snorted back to consciousness.

"Wha?" he demanded groggily.

"Wake up, Sleeping Beauty, we have a game to play," she announced.

He sat up in the semi-darkness, rubbing his eyes. "Game?" he repeated. "What are you talking about?"

"Yesterday was a fiasco," she announced firmly.

Charlie cleared his throat and didn't meet her gaze.

"But I have a solution," she continued. "Get a shower, get dressed, and meet me out on the boardwalk in half an hour."

Without waiting for a reply, she walked out the door, slammed it again, and was gone.

* * *

The sun, even at dawn, was a blinding beacon which shimmered water, heated air, and reflected sand like glass. Donning the $10 pair of sunglasses he'd bought the day before, Charlie scanned the boardwalk (new, he thought disapprovingly; *different*), and finally located his wife at the far end, where the last stairway down to the beach met a drift of white sand.

"What are those?" he asked, nodding at two somethings in his wife's hands.

"What do they look like?"

"Hey." Charlie leaned close. "These... how?"

"I went for a walk this morning," Sarah said. "All over town. Up streets, down lanes, between buildings, through alleys. And in one of the alleys, right behind the new Gap, in fact, I found an old pile of junk. Some fake green turf, an old model lighthouse… and a couple of beat-up golf clubs and two golf balls, one blue, one red."

"I remember these," he murmured.

Sarah nodded. "Here." She handed him a club. "And here." She handed him the red ball.

"How'd you know I always chose red?" he asked.

"You painted the outside of our house red," she said shortly. "The whole damn thing. Let's go down to the shore."

They walked out onto the beach until their feet touched damp sand.

"The 18th hole," said Sarah. She dropped her ball. "Par One. You ready?"

A slow, hesitant smile played across Charlie's face. He dropped his ball in the sand beside hers.

"Ready?" Sarah repeated.

"Yes. Yes! Ready."

They swung. The balls disappeared far out to sea, each plying a brief hole in the vast, golden expanse. Then they were gone.

"Hole in one!" exclaimed Sarah. "Two of them!"

Charlie looked out at the sea for a long, long time before turning to his wife.

"Breakfast?" he asked.

Sarah nodded. "If you're interested, there's this new restaurant called Bethany Bayou."

"Sounds great. You know, suddenly I could eat a *horse*."

A few hours later, the tide came in and took the two clubs.

Just Beneath

The day had been hot and humid, as most late-August days in central Maryland are, and with summer almost over and the smell of chalk and musty 8th grade textbooks haunting their future, the three boys looked for something to fill the evening that would remind them of the season all but done and past.

It was Scott Cleary who thought of going to the lake at Centennial Park, and Tim Wilson who agreed it was a good idea.

"We can get popsicles and go canoeing," said Tim. "I love canoeing. You can outrace other people and cut from one end of the lake to the other. Yeah, I'm in. Let's do it!"

That left Ron Atkins, who suddenly found himself under the scrutinizing gaze of his friends.

"You in, Ron?" Tim asked.

"Why don't we just go to the basketball courts?" said Ron. "There's a whole ton of stuff to do at the park besides splash around on the lake."

"We played basketball last night," said Scott.

"Rollerblading?"

"Boring," Tim said, voice flat. "And besides, my blades are busted."

Ron sighed, sensing a losing battle. Then genius struck. "I got a pack of Camels from my brother. We can go in the woods by the dock and smoke 'em. I just gotta run home first and sneak 'em out."

This did cause Scott and Tim to pause, but only for a moment. "No time," said Scott. "The sun's going down and they stop renting canoes at dusk. We'll smoke 'em tomorrow."

And that was that. Ron glanced around Scott's basement—at the flat-screen TV, the stack of Blu-ray discs, the paintball equipment carefully mounted on the far wall, the framed jersey worn by Cal Ripken at a game in 1992—then looked back to Scott and Tim, who were already pocketing money, iPhones, and keys for the walk.

And he suddenly realized, for the first time, that Scott's family had money, and Tim's didn't, and what that meant. He wondered if Scott knew why Tim always said "yes" to everything he suggested. Hell, he'd only just figured it out himself.

"Come on, Ron," said Scott. They were going with or without him. He could go to the lake or go home.

Bemused, he followed his old friends up the stairs.

* * *

"Why you want to keep away from the lake, anyhow?" Tim asked, flipping Ron's baseball hat off his head and taking a bite of cherry Popsicle. They were sitting on the dock by the canoes, waiting for the attendant to bring oars.

"It's boring, that's all," said Ron, replacing his hat and slugging Tim's arm.

"I know," said Scott. "It's about the guy who drowned here last week. Isn't it?"

Scott knew Ron well. That had always been a strength in their friendship, but sometime, at some point—Ron couldn't tell exactly when, but recently—that strength had turned into something else.

"No, that's not it," Ron said flatly.

But Tim picked up the torch and said, "You don't like deep water, do you, Ron? I mean, you don't go swimming. I never seen you in the pool, only dangling your feet. You *ever* swim?"

"He doesn't know how," said Scott.

"I do," Ron retorted.

"Only the doggie-paddle."

The attendant handed each of them an oar, watched as they latched on their lifejackets, and helped them push off from the dock. “An hour ‘till we close,” she said, then walked back to the stand.

Tim threw his Popsicle stick over his shoulder. Ron watched as it landed in the water and floated, suspended on the surface. The lake, always muddy, had been the first thing to darken in the encroaching twilight, and he wondered how many feet of that darkness now wallowed and flowed beneath them.

“You’re still thinking about the guy who drowned,” Scott repeated. “Isn’t that right? It’s making you nervous?”

The oars cut through the water, causing slight ripples with every touch. Centennial Lake, wide, flat, expansive, spread out around them, reflecting the last fire of the dying day.

“It’s sad,” Ron said, sitting in the middle of the canoe, no oar, Tim before him and Scott behind him, both paddling strongly toward the center of the lake. “He was fishing in a little boat with friends, and he fell in and got tangled up in the lake weeds. That’s what they think. As simple as that. Isn’t it sad?”

Tim snorted. “What a dumbass. If he was that stupid, he deserved it.”

Ron was silent.

“I know what you mean,” Scott said, paddling as the canoe traveled farther from shore.

Ron was surprised. He turned around and stared at Scott, who was looking straight ahead. “You do?”

Scott nodded. “It’s sad, all right. Just imagine. You’re safe in a boat, surrounded by your friends. Maybe you just went out to relax, to get away from it all. The sun’s bright and warm, and you’re feeling pretty good, and maybe you feel a tug on your line, so you lean forward… and that’s all it takes. You’re up and over and into the water, and it’s cold down there, cold and lonely, and you’re all alone with everyone else safe up above. And you think to yourself, *I’ll push up to the surface. I’ll be back with everyone in just a second*, but then you try, and nothing happens, and you realize you're caught, and the more you pull, the tighter the vines hold on."

As Scott spoke, nothing interrupted him but the oars cutting through the water. Tim, besides his rhythmic rowing, was silent. Listening.

"And then you get it. You get that it's all over; that this is happening to *you*, not to someone else. That the cold and dark and loneliness is all you're ever going to have, and that the light and warmth belongs only to other people now. And then your lungs start to hurt, and the pain gets worse and worse, and you panic more and more, and everything starts to fade…"

"Stop it," said Ron. "Just stop." His voice was very small, very quiet.

And Scott did stop, and Ron knew it wasn't because he'd asked, but because Scott knew he had no need to say more. He'd said enough.

Then Tim laughed. Ron wanted to slug him, to shove him off the canoe into the dark water, but he didn't hate Tim enough for that. *No one* deserved that.

"I want to go back to shore," Ron said softly.

"I paid for the canoe, I'm getting my hour," Scott replied.

"I want to go back to shore," Ron repeated.

Tim laughed a second time—a rolling, high giggle. "Hear that, Scott? Ron wants to go back to shore. He's scared."

Ron once again looked back at Scott. Scott was smiling. Smirking, more like. And at that moment Ron realized Scott hated him, that the friendship had survived only as a remnant from a gone time, that it existed only as routine, that nothing deep or true remained behind it. He knew Scott and Scott knew him, and Scott, knowing him, now wanted him gone… and had all the ammunition he needed to make that desire a reality.

"There's no reason to be scared, Ron," Scott said, still paddling. "You've got a life jacket on, and the fisher guy didn't. You couldn't drown in this lake now if you tried. And as for the dead, they can't hurt you. Once he stopped breathing he became just another log. He'll turn up soon enough, I'll bet, and then—"

"Wait," Ron said. "Wait."

Scott waited.

"You mean…"

Scott waited some more.

"You mean he's…still down there?"

"Oh, c'mon, man, you knew that. They've been diving for the body over and over, and no luck. Probably stopped for the day just before we got here, come to think of it."

And suddenly Ron felt a creeping horror—a stealthy, sickening panic. He closed his eyes and grabbed both sides of the canoe. He breathed in, out, in, out, fast and faster, and then his gorge rose up in a big, hot rush, and over the side it all came out…

And as he vomited, he thought, *Scott knew that, too. How I got scared after seeing Grandma dead. About how ever since, thinking about seeing dead bodies makes me sick. I told him that at a birthday sleepover when we were nine, and I cried 'cause I was ashamed, and he cheered me up by getting me an extra piece of cake, though I didn't feel up to eating it…*

Scott turned the canoe around. Tim protested but they headed straight to shore. And the whole way, Ron kept his eyes firmly shut and his hands firmly clamped to either side of the canoe, even as Scott said, "Hey, I was only kiddin' around, Ron. There's no body still down there. They found him an hour later. I was only kiddin' around…" Even as Tim told puking stories of his own to try and make Ron feel better. Even as they both said that basketball sounded fine, just fine…A night game, maybe?

“Not tonight,” said Ron, once they were back on the dock and his stomach had settled. “I’m just gonna go on home.”

“All right,” said Tim. “Maybe tomorrow.”

“Hey, I’m sorry,” added Scott. Ron couldn’t make out his expression in the dark. “I didn’t mean to freak you out so much.”

“It’s fine, I don’t care,” Ron said. But as he turned away and headed home in the muggy summer night, he felt very cold and very alone.

Come True

Jen was enjoying the Friday afternoon: the reprieve from students, the cheap merlot, the late-day autumn sunlight. Gloria's back deck was high up in the trees, and the bright leaves rustled in the cool, light wind. It was a time for thinking about nothing with any great passion; a time for unwinding and drinking wine and eating tortilla chips with mild salsa. October was a long month—no days off, a slew of papers to grade—and such breaks were to be cherished.

Then Tara said, "It's Jen's birthday next Tuesday, you know. We should do something."

Jen coughed. Gloria laughed.

"What's so funny?" Tara asked, crunching another chip.

"How did you find out about Jen's birthday?" Gloria asked. "She keeps that date pretty well guarded."

"It was on the faculty page of the school's website. They're all on there."

Jen smiled faintly.

"What's the big deal?" Tara prodded. "We don't have to celebrate how *old* you are. It's just that it's your special day. And besides, you can't be more than…"

"Twenty-seven," Jen answered softly. "I'll be twenty-seven."

"This is your first year," Gloria said, shaking her head at Tara in mock consternation. "Otherwise you'd have known that birthdays make Jen nervous. She has a complex about them. Don't ask her to explain."

For Jen, all the color had drained from the autumn leaves, and the gentle wind, soothing up until a moment ago, now seemed tinged with menace and the sweet, pervasive scent of decay. One blink, and the afternoon was ruined. "Why not?" she said. "I can explain it very well, if I want to."

Gloria grunted, sipping her wine. "But in four years, you never have."

"You said you'd never bring it up."

Gloria swirled her wine in its glass. "I didn't," she said simply. "Tara did."

And then, for the first time in almost two decades, anger got the best of Jen's common sense. *Catty*, she thought, then turned to Tara. "Do you want to know why I don't like birthdays?"

"Um… yes. No. I mean, not if it's going to upset you. I didn't mean—"

"No, no, you didn't do anything." Jen cast a quick glance at Gloria, who met her gaze without blinking.

"It's very simple," Jen said.

* * *

There was a party. A *great* party, all planned and orchestrated with meticulous care by Jenny's mother. She loved turning Jenny's birthday parties into immense, time-consuming projects, and the end-results of her efforts always met with success.

This year, the theme was *My Little Pony*—the current fad for seven year-old girls—and the house had been decorated accordingly. Jenny, dressed in her best, looked around, thrilled at the glittered floor paths, the sparkling pony banners, the pastel-colored pony doll at each place on every table. All of the other dozen girls were thrilled (but not Davy Perkins, it must be said; his mother had made him come), screaming and shrieking from one game to the next, but none more than Jenny herself.

It was a perfect day.

It was *her* day.

Even outside, even in October, the sun shone warm, compliant with the needs of the occasion. So eventually the party moved to the back porch, and then out to the back yard, where the great apple tree grew up to cover the cool grass and fallen, gently rotting apples in shifting shade and cascading leaves.

They raced around the trunk, all the girls and even Davy, holding their ponies, pretending to *be* ponies, running, then trotting, then galloping through the grass. And Jen felt free, and happy, and special, and thought of the presents waiting on the table inside, the ice cream, the cake, and everyone singing "Happy Birthday"...

And then Debbie Wilson, who lived three doors up, tripped her.

It was on purpose. Jenny saw Debbie's leg come out, felt Debbie's foot turn up to catch her ankle, and then she was falling, arms pinwheeling, to sprawl in a patch of rotten apples that left her white dress streaked with pulp, dirt, and grass stains and her left knee bloodied.

She didn't cry. Not yet. First she looked up, saw Debbie running away, saw Debbie laughing, saw Debbie glance back and continue on around the tree...

"Debbie did it," she told her parents moments later. But Debbie said no, no, she hadn't, she hadn't touched Jenny at all, and that's when Jenny started to cry—but Debbie started crying too, and she cried *louder* than Jenny, so Jenny's parents appeased her by saying it had all been a "big accident."

Ten minutes later, things were calm again—Jenny changed and cleaned up, Debbie smiling and laughing, all the girls (and even Davy) happily streaming back into the house for cake and ice cream.

But Jenny was still angry—*very* angry—despite her smile. And when her mother brought out the cake, candles a great wall of cheery light, she knew what she would wish for when she blew them out.

When the children finished singing, Jenny smiled, and it was genuine this time, and she was looking right at Debbie.

Then she blew out the candles. All seven of them. In one breath pulled from deep in her lungs.

And Debbie dropped dead.

* * *

There was a pregnant silence.

It was Tara who finally laughed nervously. "You're joking!"

"No." Jen shook her head. "I wished that she would die, and she did. Five seconds later."

"Coincidence," Gloria whispered, then repeated the word louder, with more certainty. "Coincidence."

"Sure," agreed Tara. "Yes, of course it was."

"They said it was an aneurysm. A ticking time bomb just waiting to go off. No one could have known, and there were no symptoms." Jen shook her head and looked down into her wine glass.

Silence again. Then Tara cleared her throat. "Why did Debbie trip you?"

"Who can say? Children do things without thinking. They have flashes of meanness, same as adults. We'd always been good friends. For that matter, why did I wish her dead? Same reason, I guess."

"And all these years…" Tara trailed off.

Jen took up the line. "I've kind of blamed myself. At first, consciously. Then, as the years passed and I came to recognize how unlikely it all was, I knew on a rational level that I wasn't to blame, but I still felt guilty. Because deep down, I still believed I'd caused it to happen. Knowing and feeling are two different things, you see."

Gloria exhaled audibly. "Wow. What a story! No wonder. It must have been very hard, living with that. So no more parties, no more celebrations."

"Not since I was seven. Not a single one." Jen's lower lip quivered almost imperceptibly, then stilled. "But you know, I'm glad you brought it up, I really am."

Gloria arched her eyebrows. "Really?"

"Yes. I think talking about it made me realize how silly it is. And it would be a good, healing experience, to have a birthday party again… to help me put it behind me once and for all. Don't you think?"

"Oh, absolutely!" said Tara. "Sure it would!"

"Yes," agreed Gloria more quietly. "Yes, I agree."

"I can plan the whole thing," said Tara. "I'll get the cake, send out invitations. We can make it as large or small a party as you'd like! And I'll figure out who can bring what, and we'll throw you a 'Welcome back to Birthday Parties' birthday party. Oh, it'll be great!"

"That's so sweet of you," Jen said. "It really will help me put all this behind me. Of course," she added, almost as an afterthought, "it's hard to destroy *every* doubt. I think there will probably always be some small part of me that will wonder if I really had something to do with… no, but enough of that!" She sipped her wine and swallowed, enjoying the dry taste that somehow complimented the great spray of autumn colors that surged around them.

"What should I bring?" Gloria said. She didn't look at Jen as she spoke.

Tara opened her mouth to say something, but Jen beat her to it. "You've already done so much, Gloria. You made this possible by talking about it, even when you knew I didn't want you to. But it was for the best, and I thank you for that."

She pursed her lips, thinking.

"The *candles*," she said at last, snapping her fingers. "Gloria, you just bring the candles. That'll be plenty."

"Yes! A cake has to have candles," said Tara brightly.

Gloria fixed her gaze on Jen, who met it without blinking. "That… that will be fine," she murmured.

"Great! And I know just what to wish for," Jen said, taking another sip of wine before reaching out and patting Gloria's cold, cold hand.

To Be

His name was Allan Eden, and he moved about in darkness absolute except for the stars.

As far as he could tell, the land before him had once supported his home. It was desolate now; charred, hard earth indistinguishable from the rest of the wasteland that extended for miles in every direction. He could see little in the blackness save the glint of mica chips and the outline of rough-hewn rock, but thought nothing of waiting the long hours until daybreak. He had plenty of time.

Allen Eden was lonely. He was also dead. Yet the loneliness was not that which most of the dead-and-left had felt since humanity's first tentative steps in the metaphorical garden that was his namesake. It was a loneliness the depth and breadth of which few had ever experienced, and none with any sense would wish to.

For the multitude, death was not so bad. Many enjoyed it, Eden thought with bitterness. But he had died under violent circumstances, and although the theories of the living rarely came close to approaching the true nature of life after death, some few individuals had embraced one during his lifetime that had turned out to be disconcertingly true: those who died unhappily, and under certain traumatic conditions, were bound indefinitely to the mortal plane: ghosts. And ghosts, in Eden's experience, were all unhappy. Some people who truly loved life remained partially behind after their body's demise to cherish the world a short time longer before moving on, but they weren't *true* ghosts: a healthy portion of their being had already achieved transcendence, and only a vague essence remained for a time before joining it. *True* ghosts, the "lifers" as one of his incorporeal companions once ironically termed it, were in the majority, and they all suffered.

To Eden, it seemed the time immediately following death was cheerless for ghosts, either because of the paths their lives had taken, or because of the way those paths had ended: a secret shame, a raging regret, murder, a car accident, drowning; any facet of life or death that made moving on seem more impossible than the suffering which thrust them into ghosthood to begin with. The instinctual need to *remain*, to make right, was very difficult for the Afterworld to reconcile; thus, it often did not. If strong enough, need could overwhelm the natural beck and call of higher dimensions, and Eden's need was very great.

Looking up at the bright, distant light of the stars and planets, he sighed, and the sigh was such that a thin wind sprang up in a cyclonic eddy before him and moved off down the barren plain. Unhappiness was not stationary: the range of its levels was great, and one manifestation could quickly take the place of another, or, even worse, join with it as two strong brothers often join up against a less fortunate only child.

He thought of the second manifestation of his sadness: how, gradually, once the sting of his own murder had worn off, the uneasy, hollow desire for revenge began to gnaw at his thoughts. Roughly two years after his death, Eden had visited his knife-handy wife for the first time since his funeral. Preparing for bed, Sarah had opened the bedroom closet to grab a bathrobe, and shaken hands with his cold, clammy hand instead. Her scream was music to his ears, and for the next fifty-seven years Eden enjoyed the various ranges Sarah's worn vocal chords could achieve when frightened. When she finally expired at the respectable age of ninety-three, having outlived the integrity of most of her vital organs by a number of years, his former wife had been near-catatonic for over a decade and raving mad for another before that, locked away in an asylum on the outskirts of Baltimore.

Yet following the conclusion of his vigorously-undertaken revenge, loneliness set in, as it does for all who don't belong where they are. Figuring eternity was a long time to deal with depression without Prozac, therapy, or even the option of suicide, Eden began devising ways to cheer himself.

* * *

Eden struck a hard, pocked deposit that lay near the tips of his phantasmic tendrils. It clattered unevenly down the barren plain, kicking up sharp, orange sparks. He waited while the sound faded, the sparks went out, and the rock fell still again. He had been around so long, learned so much, that the ability to move physical objects was ingrained, like breathing had once been.

He thought again of Sarah, and how long it had been since their last post-death encounter. She had come to him just a few weeks after losing grip of her body, sane again and mad as hell. If looks could kill! Eden had never witnessed such concentrated vitriol. He attempted to flee but could think of no place to hide from another free-ranging ghost like himself. Sarah and her envenomed spirit-tongue followed him across the continental United States, over the Atlantic, and eventually caught up with him among the ancient-timbered buildings of London, in the famous Drury Lane Theatre, among the spirits of antiquity and during a somewhat under-produced production of *All's Well That Ends Well.* Then, as he stood before her blistering, withering onslaught of words, he realized something: it was good having her around again.

Upon seeing that her presence brought Eden happiness, however, Sarah quickly calmed and became one of the few purgatorial spirits to ascend to the Great Beyond, delayed peace serving as the key to her transcendence. In leaving him, she exacted the only form of retribution that could actually cause Eden pain. The loneliness began to bite harder.

Other spirits were difficult to talk to. The cynical and resentful generally tire of the happy and content, so Eden found the short-term "benevolent" presences not only boring, but often downright annoying. They kept trying to convince him to lighten up, sometimes quite eloquently, but simply didn't understand the nature of his situation. As for the other "lifers," for the most part all they did was complain, gossip, and sulk. He avoided almost all of them, save for a brief conversation now and again, and they him.

That left Eden with the living to toy around with. For years innumerable he haunted the darker avenues of the world, inhabiting everything from the undersides of Eastern-European stone bridges and the attics of campus dormitories in the American Mid-West, to cursed glades in the African wild and various unlucky passes in the Himalayas. For a time, he enjoyed the startled, fearful, and sometimes worshipful reactions that his moans, brief appearances, or icy touches invoked. But one day, after inadvertently causing the infant son of a young Queensland woman to burst into tears, the mother, bath-robed, face-creamed, and already well aware of his hauntings, actually *screamed* at him. Spinning around the room in circles, unable to see him yet obviously feeling his presence, she shrieked, "Jealous! Pathetic! That's what you are. Leave us alone and take it somewhere else!" Then, before leaving the room to calm the baby in the kitchen, she slowly, deliberately, *gave him the finger.*

Eden never bothered the living on purpose again. He was too offended.

He took, instead, to learning about the universe. For this task, Time, at least momentarily, was on his side. He read everything of scientific value that interested him. He visited museums, watched operations, looked over the shoulders of geniuses at work. He conducted as much field research as he could manage. He learned meditation and studied all the major philosophies. He immersed himself in theology (having an interesting personal perspective to aid him), numerology, and, for the hell of it, philology. His memory, improved by immateriality, acted as an information dump of almost limitless proportions. It took millennia, but by the time his lust for information was sated, Eden had proven the existence of no less than 26 dimensions; come to understand how a universe could exist without a beginning and without an end; expanded upon the theories of Einstein, Hawking, and two dozen others until discovering their ultimate cruxes; determined the logical meaning of life; discovered the logical meaning of death; debunked the concept of finity; and cured the common cold (imparting the cure to the living through automatic writing with a primary school mistress in Iceland).

Then, despite his labors toward enlightenment, a familiar darkness once again began to steal into Eden's sight, and this time it seemed to whisper, faintly, of an even greater darkness yet to come. Time, so integral to his studies, slowly, once again, became his curse.

* * *

All those experiences, all those memories, were from years long ago, when the concept of years was still embraced by others besides himself. Now Eden, his presence permeating the site of his old home and ancient life, tried hard not to think about time. He felt the rare, yet growing fear of what a close review of his post-body existence would do to him. He knew his sanity, or at least its spiritual equivalent, had been growing increasingly fragile for ages, so he tried to avoid unnecessary provocations that might accelerate its decline.

Thinking too much about the present didn't help, either. Eden did not wish to consider how long it had been since he had seen a living man or woman. The last rocket had left for a better world eons ago, leaving him behind, trapped by the rules of the afterlife to haunt the globe the way some unlucky souls were confined to the site of a former building, lake, or forest. The strange animals that evolved as the sun aged and grew (vast beasts with skins of radiation-proof bone, tiny mammalian imps that chattered on the shores of the Great Sea) only perpetuated his loneliness. Their appearance, like the changes in the planet's geography, evoked within him a penetrating, profound sense of melancholy. Even most of the ghosts were now of species he didn't know or understand.

The weather, too, had shifted with the ages. Eden missed snow, and in the more recent past had often ascended the diminishing white-capped mountains or floated above the poles to relieve the tedium of hot weather. He missed the polarities of seasons. His favorite, autumn, was difficult to forget, despite the evolution or extinction of the trees that had once characterized it with falling leaves and colored brilliance, and despite that he had felt neither hot nor cold, wet nor dry, in a span of time that had seen half a dozen geologic ages come and go. He remembered pumpkins. Jack o' Lanterns. The smell of burning leaves and the decay of wet grass. The sound of costumed children giggling at doors. Not even photographs remained, but he remembered.

And last but not least, a final, bitter pill: the ghosts of his generation were beginning to lose their holds on reality.

Eden truly missed one of them, an old pirate named Charles Weary. Bound to the perimeter of the London tavern where he had tasted poison in the early sixteenth century, Weary had for a long while been something close to a friend. He had been a bitter soul but not as gloomy as the rest: a combination which attracted Eden. In fact, Weary hadn't even been above cracking a joke, although the old favorites had worn a bit thin after a few thousand years. Yet slowly, almost unnoticeably, his behavior had changed. On one memorable occasion Weary had called him "Father," and carried on an entire (one-sided) conversation with "Father" until Eden, dismayed, made some kind of excuse and fled across the world for a few centuries. On a much later encounter, when the progression had grown more pronounced, Charles had taken Eden by his vaporous shoulders, looked him in the eye, and asked, almost pleading, "Is this Heaven? Is this Heaven?"

Immortality was cruel; immortality with its own brand of spiritual Alzheimer's doubly so.

Best not to think of it, he reminded himself.

Eden blew upon the surface of the world with cold breath. Dust and sand rose, spiraled, and returned to earth with a whisper of contact. His home had been a simple, middle-class ranch house of red brick and white vinyl siding. The kitchen, the bedrooms, the living room, the dining area: all stages for fleeting emotions, some wonderful, others certainly not. Yet they had been *his* stages, places of ultimate shelter. Now, the land had risen six thousand feet, continents had shifted, everything had changed since it had belonged to him—and ultimately these results of time now brought to his attention, as they often had before, the inarguable fact that the small square of earth hadn't actually been his at all. He'd borrowed it long ago, and it had moved on.

Eden especially missed his tiny study, filled with the photographs of four generations, journals, prints, and books that had all served to mute and relieve the less agreeable aspects of his nature: impatience, anger, frustration, stubbornness.

His struggle to understand Sarah's ultimate acts of rejection, first adultery and then murder, had ended long ago. Which of his characteristics, if any, had driven her to such lengths? How much had he been to blame for her infidelity? For her hatred? How much had been her fault, how much his? It no longer mattered. His personal discoveries had taught him that the past, unlike almost everything else, could not be changed and was beyond manipulation.

As the wind blew cold over the rocky plain, Eden's thoughts turned, unexpectedly, to Sarah's garden. He had liked working it beside her during the first years of their marriage. Tomatoes, squash, lettuce, beans; all had grown ripe and strong under their careful tending. He missed the floppy straw hat Sarah had always worn when picking cherry tomatoes. He missed the tulip pattern on her garden gloves. Pulling the wisp of his form closer together against a chill he could not feel, Eden realized he even missed the ache of poison ivy blisters, always the only penalty for sharing such work with her.

The ink of night was lifting. Dawn was near, the once-pitch sky now a lightening ochre. Soon the red sun would rise, burning away the clouds to provide him an unobstructed view of its mighty, bloated majesty and the barren land beneath. The mold spoors that spread during the night withered, hissing, to die black and burnt, the meager remains leaving their cannibalistic descendants a form of shelter and sustenance in which to grow and reproduce when night came again.

"A new day," he muttered, thinking of poison ivy blisters, the lovely feel of the hurt and itch, and Sarah's careful administration of calamine lotion. "A new day."

Suddenly he paused, mind racing, scared. Poison ivy. Sarah's garden. Her hat. Sarah's gloves. Sarah's…

Sarah's face.

He couldn't remember it.

He stood motionless for a long time, the sun rising higher and higher in the white sky until it burned down directly overhead, scalding the land beneath him. Still he thought. Still no face came to him.

Finally, Eden looked at the sky, the ground, the horizon. Move on, he told himself. Move on and think later. To the south waited the tropics, lush jungles and warm rivers mocking paradise with visceral, dangerous life. To the north, desolation. East? The salt flats. West, the mountain ranges. And always waiting somewhere ahead and beyond, in every direction, was the sea.

Eden began to spin, fast, fast, faster, until he was oblivious to direction, the world a blur around him. When he stopped, he stopped suddenly, randomly. Everything was very quiet. Nothing living cried and there was no longer any wind. If he could have done so, he would have closed his eyes. If he could have done so, he would have slept. Instead, he began to move, not caring what lay ahead, the purpose of his thought like a vast, dark garden bearing fruit he knew, eventually, would have to be consumed.

The Key

"Again."

"Yes. Again."

The two men, both on the far side of middle age, stared at the abandoned house from the safety of the sidewalk. At their feet, on the edge of the overgrown front lawn, what had once been a cat lay rigid and desiccated, lips pulled back in a rictus sneer.

Richard Hawthorne spit.

Emil Braddock sighed.

"Something should be done," said Hawthorne.

"And what," said Braddock, "do you propose?"

Hawthorne stubbed the toe of his shoe against the cracked edge of the walk. "Well, Mayor, I have a couple ideas. Both involve demolition."

"Demolition involves people demolishing," Braddock said impatiently. "No one will do it. We've been *over* this. For years and *years*, we've been over this."

"We could hire people from out of town," Hawthorne continued. "They'll value the work."

"I can't have that on my conscience, Dick." Braddock looked up at the darkening sky. "Here, it's almost sunset. Let's go to Schooner's and grab a beer. I don't want to see her again."

"No. No, we can't have that. No. Me neither."

* * *

For years 101 Sycamore had been an unassuming house. Then, sometime during the course of its long history, things had taken a bad turn. The place was old and had been rented out as flats around the turn of the century, so the exact circumstances of the problem were hard to pinpoint. Too many people had lived there, and records were scarce. But shortly before half the men in town left for World War I, the house began to develop a reputation. By the time the surviving doughboys returned, it was abandoned.

And shunned.

Hawthorne took a pull of beer and sighed. "You know whose cat that was, Emil?"

Braddock nodded. "Your granddaughter's. Yes, I'm well aware. We've *all* lost pets to it, Dick. You can't take it personally."

Hawthorne leaned forward. "It's not about *taking it personally*, goddamn it. It's about taking care of this problem *once and for all.* The children of this town should be able to grow up without having to pay for therapy later! They should—"

"Lower your voice."

Hawthorne looked around. "Sorry," he said, addressing Schooner's few other patrons, then turned back to his drink. "It's just… this town is *dying*, Emil. When the kids grow up they move away and don't come back."

"That happens in lots of small towns, especially when the mines close."

"But we all know it happens more in Still Creek. And we all know why."

They were silent, both ruminating on encounters they wished to forget. After dark, the ghost that haunted 101 Sycamore was indiscriminate—it appeared to whoever happened to be passing by—staring out this window, leering out that, peering from the rotting cupola. One didn't forget the sight.

And then there were the animals.

The house, as anyone who chose to venture near quickly discovered, was invariably ringed with dead birds, squirrels, rabbits and chipmunks. Sometimes the bodies of fox, deer, dogs, and cats could also be seen, slowly putrefying in the brown, knee-high grass and weeds. And beneath them, like rotting strata, was layer after layer of desiccated skin, matted fur, and weather-stained bones.

"I saw it when I was seven." Hawthorne emptied the last of his pint and clunked the glass down on the scarred table. "That was the first time. I remember like it was yesterday. So many memories fade but that one doesn't. That says something, huh?"

Braddock grunted.

"I was walking home from Johnny Crane's. Remember him? Killed in the war? Well, he had a late birthday party. It was a *great* party. I'd won a goldfish. Dark had fallen and on I walked, poking at the bag, not heeding anything else, and before I knew it that damned house was on my left and I happened to glance up. And there she was, standing on the front porch. Her body glowed. She had on a mildewed white dress. Her arms were folded across her chest like a corpse in a coffin, and they were beastly thin, and her hair was all tangled and wet. And her eyes—"

"Oh shut up, Dick. I know about the eyes. We all do."

"There *were* no eyes, just huge, gaping sockets. And the lips were gone—her mouth a big, bloodless gash for her teeth to poke through."

Braddock shook his head. Once Hawthorne started, all you could do was be patient and let him finish.

"Well, I stood there a moment, thinking it was some kind of prank, then remembered the stories, all those horrible stories, and that's when she opened her mouth and shrieked.

"I dropped the goldfish. I remember the splat, the water gushing out on the sidewalk and the fish flapping around silently, pulling in air, dying, and then I ran. I ran like never before. I ran and I ran, on and on, until I slammed through the front door of my house and started hollering to wake the dead. Daddy had to throw a blanket over me and tackle me to the floor before I calmed.

"For weeks following I woke up screaming, night after night. Seeing her, it deadened the world for me. Every time I started enjoying something I remembered her, remembered that *shriek*, and all the fun went out of it. I wasn't the same for years. And Emil, little Barney Stover saw her just last week. He's only *five years old*, Emil. *Think* of it."

Braddock rubbed his eyes with his thumb and forefinger. "Maggie Stover was an idiot, taking her boy for a walk at dusk—never a brain in that pretty head of hers. I've always said so." He paused. "It doesn't do good to talk of it. Talk's cheap. There's nothing we can do."

"You're right. Talk *is* cheap. People want a man of action, and you're mayor of this town. Haven't you heard the grumbles? Unless I'm mistaken, there's an election coming up and Sam Kolbrenner's chomping at the bit for a piece of you. It'd pay to listen to me."

That silenced Braddock. Glowering, he sat back.

"No demolition," continued Hawthorne. "No out-of-town contractors. Fine. I understand. That leaves one option."

"What?" Braddock said, looking like he'd just sucked a lemon.

"Let's you and me head on down to the gas station."

* * *

Wheezing and out of breath, Braddock and Hawthorne crouched behind a dead bush in the deepening twilight.

"I don't see how this is going to get me re-elected," Braddock growled. "I'm more likely to be arrested. Imagine what Kolbrenner would do with *that*."

"A good deed doesn't go unnoticed," Hawthorne replied, fiddling with the cap of his gas can. "Word spreads through odd channels. The town will thank you."

"Sure, sure. You take the front of the house. I'll take the back. And for God's sake, make it quick and keep your eyes down. If that thing appears on the porch, I'll shit myself."

"That'll make two of us."

"Go."

They went.

Ten minutes later, a warm, bright glow flickered all down Sycamore Street and outshone the full moon.

* * *

"It's gone, Mayor. Every bit of it."

Emil Braddock stood on the sidewalk staring up at the smoldering ruins. A crowd milled around with him, over a hundred all told. *Like a nice day at the fair,* he thought. *Should I make a speech?*

Truth be told, he felt like it. He felt *good.* As he looked at the faces in the crowd—familiar, all of them—he saw nothing but relief, quiet pleasure… and approval. They couldn't know, could they? But like Hawthorne said, "Word spreads through odd channels."

"Yes, it's gone," he replied, turning to Mrs. Perkins, the old lady who'd had the misfortune of living in 103 Sycamore for over two decades. "You have nothing to worry about now, Dorothy. Nothing at all. You can pull the boards off your western windows and walk down the street on warm summer nights." He smiled. "This is one fire I can't feel too awfully bad about."

The relieved chuckle that went up from the crowd stayed with him all day and into the evening. It sustained him, lulled him, perked him up and pleased him.

Late in the evening, after a relaxing supper, he called Hawthorne to tell him about it—to tell him about how he'd been *right*—and to thank him.

He smiled, thinking how surprised Hawthorne would be. Braddock hardly ever said "Thank you," so people knew that when he did, it really meant something.

But Hawthorne didn't answer.

"Funny," he said, and stumped back down the hall to the living room as the sirens from the fire station began to wail. Hawthorne *always* answered his phone after dark; he never went out, unless with him. And the fire station? They never conducted drills after sundown. A real fire, just a day after the one he'd set? What were the odds?

His ruminations were cut short by a startled yell, then a scream, then a dog barking frantically before yelping and falling silent.

"Something," he murmured in his darkened house, "isn't right."

Another noise, persistent and severe: frantic pounding on the front door. Bemused, Braddock answered it.

"We never thought!" Hawthorne said, hair wild, eyes wilder.

"Get in here, dummy, and calm down."

"No! Not in there. Not *anywhere.* We have to leave!"

"What are you talking about? What's going on?"

Braddock stepped out onto his porch. The whole town seemed to be coming alive in what should have been a quiet, peaceful night: lights blinking on, doors slamming, a scream, a cry, the screeching of brakes…

"*Every animal dead in every house, every yard, every field!*"

"What! *What?*" Braddock dragged the frantic, protesting man inside and shut the door.

"It's loose," Hawthorne panted, hand over his heart. "Burning it? We were wrong, Braddock. All that smoke, all that ash. I didn't think! It landed… why, it landed *everywhere.*"

Braddock's eyebrows furrowed. His lips pulled back. Then his face went slack.

"You mean—"

Hawthorne's eyes widened, focusing on something over Braddock's left shoulder. His lips turned blue. Silently, almost gracefully, he collapsed.

"You mean," Braddock continued, voice surprisingly calm, "that instead of destroying it, we gave it the Key to the Town."

He sighed. Something rustled behind him.

"This doesn't bode well for Election Day," he muttered.

Braddock turned around.

Seventeen

Seventeen years. He didn't know where to begin, so he began with Google, typing in her name and the last address he had. She and her family were long gone. Then the college she'd attended. Nothing. Then the city nearby. Still nothing, and God knew where she lived now. She was probably married, too. If so, her old name wouldn't be much help anyway.

Memories flood back at strange times. Michael knew that. Married six years, father to a three-month-old son, and suddenly, or perhaps slowly but insidiously, his thoughts had shifted back to the past. High school. The summer before he started college. And those first few months of new classes in a great, strange place where beginnings had ushered in endings and the future, quietly but irrevocably, had begun to narrow.

"You're online an awful lot now," Zola said, walking into the garage he'd converted into a den a few years before. "Want to come say goodnight to Danny and watch *Extreme Home Makeover* with me?"

He looked up from his laptop with a sigh, surprised by how much the interruption annoyed him.

"Sure. I'll be right up."

"Does that mean one minute or twenty?"

"I said I'll be right up."

The hunt hadn't started as an obsession, and he wasn't certain it had actually become one now, but certainly an urgency had crept into his searching since Danny's birth. Instead of merely checking his email and CNN.com when he went online, Michael often spent his rare free time searching old lists, class reunion bulletins, Facebook postings, and business profiles. Even as potential leads led nowhere, the memories that the hunt brought forward remained vivid for the first time in a generation—a catalyst between the years which left behind a dull, lasting ache that rose up throughout his busy days.

"Swenson," he typed into Facebook for the tenth time as the baby began to cry upstairs. "Mary Swenson."

Four dozen matches came up. A fourth of them had photographs, none of which were hers. The others were too young, too old, or had no information posted beside them. As before. As always.

Sighing again, he closed up the computer and went to change Jacob's diaper.

Afterward, he fell asleep on the chair across from his wife half an hour before Ty Pennington asked a happy, newly-saved family to yell out, "Move That Bus!" When he woke up, she was already in bed asleep.

Michael was grateful.

* * *

Things took a downturn in the weeks that followed. Of that there could be no doubt, however much Michael and Zola tried to ignore it.

Finally, one evening after a silent dinner, Zola said, "You don't like the baby."

She might as well have slapped him in the face.

"That's ridiculous," he said sharply. "I can't believe you said that. Why? Why would you even *think* that?"

"Because you don't tuck him in. You let me hold him most of the time. You resent changing him or feeding him." Tears formed in her eyes but her anger kept them from falling. "For years you talked about how much you wanted this, and now that you have it, you don't."

"That's ridiculous," he repeated. "Simply ridiculous. And malicious, too. I can't believe you have the *nerve*…"

Zola left the room, leaving him with racing thoughts and a profound silence.

In that silence, Michael realized that despite his denial, Zola had a point. There was something about the baby that bothered him. Not the baby itself, but in *having* one. Something that had caught him off guard and left him without the faintest idea of what to do.

Going to the bathroom and pressing a damp washcloth to his face, Michael looked in the mirror. What he saw shocked him: thinning hair, beginning to gray at the temples, and the start of a sagging double-chin. It made him think of something—some*one.*

He knocked on the locked bedroom door. "I'm going to see my father," he said. He waited for an answer, but none came.

* * *

"Calling me out for a beer at ten o'clock at night? What you do, lock yourself out of the house?"

Michael smiled in spite of himself. "No, just looking for some answers."

"No one ever found them in the bottom of a glass," the old man said, lifting his mug. "But as the barflies all say, it never hurts to look."

For several minutes they drank in silence. Michael tapped his fingernail against his glass until his father reached out a hand to stop him.

"OK, what gives?"

"Dad," said Michael. That was all that came. He tried again. "Dad."

"That's me."

"Did you ever… I mean, have you… oh, it's all so damned stupid. I don't even know what to ask. I'm wasting your time."

His father polished off his Yuengling and asked for another. "Yeah, you really know how to ruin my night. *Dateline* was on. I don't know how I'll get over missing *that* again."

He grunted. "OK, don't ask questions, just tell me what's happened."

Michael nodded. "The baby. He's three months old. I should be happy, and I *am*, but instead of wanting to spend time with him, I find myself trying to get away. And I spend all my free time on the Internet, trying to track down someone I haven't seen in years."

His father raised his eyebrows. "Who?"

He sighed. "Mary Swenson."

"Mary Swenson? Hmm… oh yeah, the girl you dated your senior year in high school? *That* Mary Swenson?"

"Yeah. That Mary Swenson."

"What's she up to?"

"I have no idea. I can't find out a thing about her. But I keep trying and I don't know why."

His father nodded, rubbing his gray beard. "Let me ask you three questions. The first two are 'yes' or 'no' questions, so they're not hard. But you have to be honest. Got it?"

Michael nodded.

"Question One: do you love your wife?"

"Of *course* I do."

"Yes or no, please."

"Yes."

"All right, then." His father took a swig of his second beer. "Question Two: do you like your job?"

"Teaching? Sure, most of the time."

"That's a 'yes.' OK, Question Three, and this is the toughie: *why* do you want to find Mary Swenson?"

Michael grunted into his mug and shook his head. "I don't know, Dad. I guess that's what I wanted to ask you."

"Just do your best."

"Because… because, well, I want to see her. I want to know what she's up to. See what she looks like. See what she's done with her life."

"Bonus question, then. When you think of Mary Swenson, what comes to mind?"

"I don't get what you mean."

His father grunted. "I mean just what I said."

Michael gazed at the scarred surface of the bar for a long time. "The Fourth of July," he said at last. "When we sat on the hill at the top of the street and watched the fireworks. And Senior Prom. And the dress she wore. And the smell of her favorite perfume. And me giving her a ten-dollar locket with a rose. And us walking by the stream in Spring Creek Park. And, oh, God, that whole *summer.* And she was *beautiful.* It was all so new. Anything was possible. It was all perfect."

He fell silent.

His father looked at him steadily. "And then, at the end of that summer, you broke up. You went away to college and she stayed behind, and you started dating someone else and so did she."

"That's right."

"And you never saw her again."

"That's right."

His father leaned in close. "I'm sixty-seven years old. I've done some stupid things, but I've learned a bit along the way, too. So here's what I'll do, for what it's worth. I'm going to give you two quotes by two of my favorite writers. You can take them or leave them, and then I want you to go home to your loving wife and cute little kiddo. Got it?"

Michael nodded.

"Then listen close…"

And the older man spoke, paused, and spoke some more.

* * *

There was a sleepless night, a restless morning, then late afternoon gave way to evening again.

After a tense dinner, Michael clomped downstairs, plopped down in front of the computer, and checked his email.

No new messages, save one.

The note was from an old high school friend, Andy Collins. Michael faintly remembered sending him a brief line a few weeks before. The reply read:

Hi, Mikey!

It's good to hear from you. So you're trying to track down Mary, huh? Believe it or not, my wife works with her in Sagaponak. She gave me Mary's email address to pass along to you. So here you go. Hope this helps and that all's well.

Andy

Below the note was the email address.

Michael, cold sweat beading his brow, clicked it. A blank email opened, addressed to Mary. He could write anything he wanted. Anything. And then seventeen years of silence would be broken by a thunderclap click of the mouse.

He paused, fingers hovering over the keyboard.

"'You can't go home again,'" his father had told him. "Thomas Wolfe. Ever read him?"

Slowly, his fingertips descended. They rested lightly on the keys. *I can try*, he thought.

His father's voice again: "Remember, 'This moment and all moments last forever.' Kurt Vonnegut."

Michael closed his eyes. His fingers trembled, knuckles white. Electric fire flowed through his nerve endings.

Time slowed.

"You can't go home again," he murmured, the words measured and cadenced, "but all moments last forever."

With a deep push, he exhaled.

His hands drew away from the keyboard.

He leaned down and turned off the computer.

"She is seventeen," he said softly. Upstairs, the baby began to cry. He headed up to help Zola tend him.

"And somewhere, to someone," he added, clicking off the light and closing the door, "so am I."

RILEY

Miss Riley's Lot

How bout when my big brother Chris took me up on Uncanny Hill during hunting season and let me watch while he and his buds shot a woman?

I was fifteen, and it was the day after Thanksgiving, and Chris, he was nineteen that year, a real bruiser who liked to drink and get in brawls around town, but he got along with me bettern most.

Well, he and Jim and Dale, that's his friends, they took me up in the woods above town, and further in, deep in, until Uncanny Hill reared up, and then Chris ran up ahead to the clearing, he had us wait, and came back and said, all breathless, "She's there, OK."

And I said, "Who's that?"

And he said, "You'll see," and nudged his pals.

We went on up the hill together until it broke clear from the woods and there was wheat all over on the top, and there was an old woman sittin on a rotten stump. She was all wrapped up in a shabby black-knit shawl and had on black stockings, and a black bonnet, a natty old black dress, and a tattered, dirty pair of black old wooden clogs. It was like she was in mournin or something, dressed up so. White hair streamed out from neath her shawl in long, thin strands. Her face, oh, it was like lookin at one of them maps with mountains on it, the kind that stick up a little. And her eyes, I remember when we got close thinkin how they musta once been green, but now was all faded, kinda olive-colored, and red round the edges.

"Well, Chris, that's Miss Riley!" I shouted.

All the other fellas laughed long and loud at that, but I can't say as I knew why, cept we wasn't supposed to say a word to her cause she was 'touched,' like they put it, and she had always kinda skeered me. She liked to clump around town now and again, but specially out in the woods and through the fields, and she muttered and laughed and smiled like there was somethin real sad and unspeakable behind those four black teeth of hers.

"You ain't frightened, now, are you Jeff?" Chris asked, nudging Dale.

"No, no, I ain't a bit."

"That's a good whelp. Now you follow close and watch real good."

So they moseyed on down to Miss Riley, me followin behind, and Miss Riley came clumpin up the hill aways to meet em, and Jim, he said, "How's it goin, Miss Riley?" And Miss Riley, she stopped and smiled that smile, then laughed, and it sounded like a squalling baby. And she said, "I'll show you a thing or two!" then turned and walked on down the hill agin to her dead ol stump and took a seat.

"Here now, whose turn is it?" Jim asked.

"I thought we said it was mine," Chris said.

"No, I don't remember that," Dale said.

"Three's better'n one!" Miss Riley piped up, and I thought to myself, *What's she runnin her gums about?* And then I found out.

"You say so," Chris said, and set his .30 caliber against her chest, just as Jim and Dale did the same.

And then I'll be damned if they didn't lift up the safeties, pull the triggers, and the world went up in smoke and thunder.

What I felt, it's kinda hard to put in words. All time, it seemed to hang on edge, and I let out a whoop! and a cry and fell on my knees as Miss Riley, she blowed backwards, knocked straight outta her shoes, and a fine red mist sprayed the ground, my brother, his buds, my face. Then Miss Riley just lay all still, her chest pretty well gone to glory, and her bones and innards all on view, and I closed my eyes and pinched my arm and tried to wake myself up, but acourse I couldn't cause I was waked already.

That then is what happened to begin with, and it's bad enough. But with my eyes still clamped shut so tight I saw stars, I next heard a rustling and a whispering and a grunt from one of the boys, and then high above it all, shrill and clear as winter water, Miss Riley's laughter.

I opened my eyes real slow, cause I didn't want to see no more, but there's no way I could keep em shut after hearing *that.* And what did I see but Miss Riley standing there in the knee-high wheat, puttin her shoes back on, balancin from one leg to another. Her hair, it was all wild cause her bonnet was knocked clean off by the blast, and her face was covered in blood, but she was alive, though I could still see her innards, and they was waving as she moved.

There's no point lyin, I passed out cold on the ground at that, and when I came to Chris was lookin down at me and shakin his head.

"Sorry bout that, fry. We didn't figure you'd take it so ruff, though it *is* a bit of a trial when you don't see it coming. But that's always been the best way to let a newby know what's goin on with Miss Riley, since no one'd believe otherwise."

I wiped my mouth and sat up. Jim and Dale were outta sight, but Miss Riley was sittin on her stump again and starin at me with those faded olive eyes of hers, smiling that hoary black-toothed grin.

"You're dead," I said, and pointed at her. "You gotta be."

"Ha!" she spat.

"You saw her chest," Chris said. "Look agin."

I peeked over, and that big old hole was still there in her gullet, but it didn't look too bad from what it was before.

"She'll get better," Chris said. "She always do."

"Come on by an do the same any time!" Miss Riley cackled at me, but I couldn't look at her again, an didn't feel too steady on my legs.

Chris put a hand on my shoulder. "Come on, let's get back to the house and go for a drive. You'll get your answers. It's time."

* * *

We got back to the house and didn't even go inside at all, but went straight for the old Model A Chris'd bought from Doc Weaver for twenty clams. And when we was inside and rolling down the road toward nowheres, Chris started talking.

"Here's the thing about Miss Riley," Chris said, staring ahead. "How old you say she is?"

"Eighty-five," I said, cause that was the oldest I could imagine.

Chris shook his head. "That end of town she lives in? Back when Grampa was a boy there was a big flood, and a heap of people died. You know that, don't you? You better, the way Gramma keeps on about it. OK, so most everything from there was either warshed away or left to rot, so nobody'd have to think about all the people that got kilt, and so they wouldn't disrespect nobody's memory by building it all up again. Except Miss Riley stayed, because she was there then, and already old, and she lived through it even though she was swept away more'n a mile. She came back when no one else did."

"That flood was almost a hundred years ago!"

Chris nodded, keeping his eyes on the road. "I ain't saying anyone gets it. And I guess you're wondering how she does it? Well she doesn't do much of nothing, as fur as I can tell. She just can't damn well lay herself down and die.

"Before Grampa passed on when you was little, he took me out for my first hunt and showed me what I showed you today. Miss Riley, she goads hunters into doin it, and finally long ago one of em did it for the first time, and ever since it's been kinda traditional-like for some of them to take a shot at her every year at the start of the season. Good luck, they say.

"But Miss Riley, I know why she keeps at em. She keeps at em cause she keeps hopin one of em will do her in right and kill her. It don't happen, though. Sometimes it takes longer and sometimes it takes shorter, but she always gets better. Even so, she won't never give up."

We was both quiet for a bit, and I watched the blue November sky meet the road as Chris kept drivin.

"How come she don't die?" I finally asked.

Chris sighed, then shook his head and wrinkled his nose. "There was talk of great sadfulness and all the kind of things you'd think'd go along with such a queer situ'ation. Somethin bout her son gettin kilt and her swearin to stay until he got back, and him not gettin back, so her stayin on and on. But now she's ready to go, and been ready for a long bit now."

"You think that's true?"

"Mebbe. But one thing I know is when folks don't get the ins and outs about any given thing, they make up somethin so they think they do. And that's what happened, I guess. But ya know what I think? I think there *ain't* always no reason for everythin. I think she don't die cause she don't die. That's her lot, jus like it's some's lot to die young. She's durn tired, has been since anyone alive's knowed her, but that's her lot."

That stuck like glue, and I come to think maybe Chris was right bout a story makin people feel better. I like to think the tales was true, meself. They give what happened to her some reason, bad or crazy besides. Better than none, for sure. But I'll never know one way or t'other, and so be it.

Chris snuck a glance at me. "So you're probably wonderin why the hell you ever need know bout all this business. Well, you've heard stories told, and at your age you'd be hearin more shortly as all that talk begins to take hold in you. And that'd be a damn shame, cause privacy's a right few don't deserve.

So most of you boys need to be told, and have it all out in the open, and understand how things is, and that way you won't need to talk bout it ever agin unless you're careful who with and when. You see how things stand?"

I guess I was starin out ahead at me and didn't say nothin fast enough, cause Chris reached over and punched my arm real hard. "You see how things stand?" he repeated.

"Yeah, I guess I see how things stand."

He nodded. "That's what I wanna hear. Now, she's harmless, I'll swear by that. She's odd but she won't hurt you. So if you wanna take a shot—"

"No!"

"That's your good choice, either way. But if you wanna keep away from her, there's a couple things you should know. First, next time you go swimming down at Uncanny's deep hole on a hot summer day, better be careful not to go too far underwater. I've heard it told she sets herself at the bottom of the pool with a rock tied to her ankle. It's her way of keepin cool, since drowning's death, and she can't die. So if you feel someone grab you, that's what it is. And if you don't want to get grabbed, use the hole downstream by the hill.

"Second, if you ever walk in the woods and see her hangin from the old oak tree over on the edge of Mr. Scot's, don't get scared. She do that sometimes, too. You just ain't ever seen it yet, but you will, if you keep on huntin.

"And third? Once in a while, usually at night, she'll climb up the library tower and take a leap. It's the highest buildin in town. She don't do that often any more, not since Sheriff Rogers had the borough add on that grate. And she usually only does it when she's been hittin the bottle, and no one in town's allowed to sell her any hard stuff anymore, neither. But you might see that, too, so it's best to keep one eye out and the other open." He paused and chuckled real dry. "That way she won't land on you."

We drove back home just in time for Ma's supper, and it was good but I didn't have much stomach for it. And Chris and me, we never spoke of Miss Riley again.

* * *

What happened after that? you might well ask. Well, time fades old frights. I had a good group of friends back then, Philip and John and Drake, and as we growed up we hunted together. Now we was good boys for the most part, even if we got in our share of trouble. Still, good or no, we was also of the age that liked to walk the line with things, and death is the biggest line of all. And so one early Saturday we was back in the woods hunting, and came up Uncanny Hill, and Miss Riley was there all right, settin on her stump, and she came up on us like she came up on my brother, and said, "You wanna go? I'll show you a thing or two!"

And so we talked a fair bit about it, then Drake went up and shot her right in the gullet.

The old woman staggered back a step, and her face screwed up in pain, and she let out a wollop of a holler, almost as loud as Drake's, but she didn't drop, and when she looked down and saw her stomach, she started laughin, then walked off like nothing much was the matter. Just as before.

"Now you's a man!" she crowed, hobbling away. "Now you's a man."

I gotta admit I shot her too when I saw her next, and the scary thing is, it felt *good* in a way I don't understand. But I can't say as I felt like a man. In fact, I kinda scared myself, doing that thing.

And so we'd see her around, and got used to the idea that she couldn't die, and life went on. She was crazy and not worth talkin to, otherwise I guess I'da tried to get a better thing goin with her. Knowing someone like that? Couldn't help but be interestin, but she never had nothing to say. And she was a bit of a creep, stalking around in woods and hiding in lakes and hangin from trees and laughing and smiling with those rotten teeth. And that's all there'd be to the story, cept for one more thing that happened a few years later.

There was a house up on Barnaby Street, about three blocks from my family's little place, empty about fifteen years. Well, fifteen years is a long time, and it started fallin down in places, but us boys used it for all kindsa things. We went even though we knowed it wasn't a safe place. There was wires and electrical fixins and rotten wood all about.

Shortly after I turned seventeen, me and my friends was up there one afternoon with some young ladies, and we was havin our own party in a way, and someone dropped a match in the wrong place. A bunch of old heavy yellow curtains caught fire, and before we knowed it we was runnin for our lives out into the open air. It was December, so I remember the cold of the day and the heat of the fire hittin each other, and then I heard the screams, but they warn't like those of us who was runnin. They was of pain, and they was from inside that house.

I was in quite a state, and my lungs was all filled with smoke, but I looked around and took in who was missing, and it was Drake. He was still inside. But I looked at the house, and knew I couldn't do a flat thing. There wasn't no way I could get back in there. The whole doorframe was blazin. All I could do was cover my ears, and cry, and watch, and wait for what I felt sure would happ'n.

And then Miss Riley showed up.

She came striding up the walk in her old black clogs, and she handed one of the cryin girls her tatty ol shawl, and there was a look in her faded eyes I never saw in nobody's before or since. "Here's sumpin I haven't tried!" she said, and she didn't stop walkin, just strode on in through the flaming door.

There was a long moment when nothin happened, except Drake's screams stopped, and we all feared the worst. But then out comes Miss Riley, and the fringe of her dress was burning, and her face was all smudged and black, but she had Drake slung over her back like a cord of wood, his legs held tight in her wiry old arms.

She dropped him down on the sidewalk, and I caught his head in my hands, and he was breathin. His face was black but it was only soot, and I guessed right it was the smoke that got him mostly, and that he'd fainted dead away. And sure enough he got better with only a few bitty burns and some black in his lungs.

But Miss Riley, she had plans. She took a deep breath, and my *lan* she looked so sad. And she looked us up and down, and then suddenly her eyes blazed bright, and they didn't look so old, and with a wide smile and a screech she ran back toward the smoking front door. A big lick of fire reached out to meet her, an a second later her white hair was nothin but burnin light, and the light wreathed around her head, and then she was gone.

We could hear her laughin for a long time, and her shadow flitted by the windows, and we could see her burnin in the flames, and then the whole house, it come down and she warn't laughin no more.

I figgered Miss Riley would come out chucklin again soon enough. She'd taken worse in her day, I thought. But when the ambulance came I was taken away to the hospital in Plumville, and didn't see no more of it. But I heard the fire department got there right fast, and it took ages to put out all the smolder, and the next mornin they dug under all the mess and rubble, and there she was, but there warn't much left, and she wasn't movin a whit. And I heard it said a great winter wind came up ahead of a storm not far behind, and it scattered her ashes all over town and beyond.

Well, it looked like the tired ol lady'd found her rest at last, and I must say I felt mighty good about it, even if town was a little less *interestin* without her in it. And Drake? He went on talkin to everyone who asked bout how she saved his life, which a course she had.

That said, I guess I was twenty when I first heard it.

Sure, it kept away for a good few years, but then there it was, and there was no hidin from it, and there still ain't. Not in town, and not in the woods, neither.

It was laughter, and it came from nowhere but the wind. Sometimes it came on fast and left quick, sometimes it seemed to circle bout the house or down the street and back and stay awhile. And sometimes it was cryin I heard, high and hard one time, soft and tired-like another. Course, it coulda been just the wind, and not sumpin else carried on it, say like ashes. The wind can be funny sometimes, soundin like a person. But how many times you ever recognize the voice? How many times it sound like it's singin through the dust of four black teeth?

So that's old Miss Riley's lot, and I guess some kinds of livin can be just as scary as dyin. Truth be told, I ain't half as scared of droppin dead now as I once was. No, not half as scared.

Time to Go Home

The movers took the last furniture out of his grandparents' house before nightfall, and then it was empty for the first time in seventy years. People had lived and died full lives, and the house had not known silence. Now it knew that, and it knew darkness.

John Haggerty shivered, feeling both on the back of his neck.

He stalked the empty halls and rooms. They didn't echo because of the worn carpets. To him, they did. But the emptiness, however it sounded, was necessary. Only now, vacant, could he gauge the true condition of the house and decide whether or not to keep it.

What he found did not please him.

A great crack ran across the archway between the living and dining rooms. The corners of the carpeted floors in the study sponged beneath prodding fingers. Dank basement timbers hosted termite borings. Reams of wallpaper sloughed off walls, freed from behind bookshelves and cabinets, the air a catalyst for dead glue to give way.

John surveyed these problems and a score of others in silence, pausing occasionally to make a note on his Blackberry or mop his face. Once finished, he stepped out into the gathering shadows of a late-June afternoon and flipped open his cell phone.

No signal. In Still Creek, there never was.

* * *

He went for a walk. He knew the streets and side-streets well, and there weren't many. A walk around Still Creek, through all byways and alleys, took only an hour. During that hour he thought, and the more he thought the more hardened his resolve became.

No one in the family felt he should buy his grandparents' house. His uncle thought the idea "sentimental nonsense," his mother "a money pit," his father "a waste"—and his wife, more bluntly, "the hallmark of a true idiot."

But as John turned onto Church Street off Main, then down to Pugh from Church, breathing in the smell of mown grass and late-afternoon backyard bonfires, he made up his mind: the house, regardless of how much it cost, would remain in the family.

He turned back onto Main Street and walked until the house came into view again. In the long-shadowed light, he half-expected to see his grandmother framed in the screen door, waiting for him like she always had, before Alzheimer's, then death had taken her away.

The sun reflected off the door's window glass.

John squinted.

The door opened.

And there she was.

* * *

"Come on in, supper's almost ready!"

Light-headed, throat dry, he stumbled up the front steps and into the house.

His grandmother stood before him, a paragon of health. Black hair, flower-print dress, apron and glasses, light hazel eyes. Seeing her now, four feet in front of him, was like finding something familiar that had been lost for years—sight and memory had to reconcile the object—the *person*—before mind and reality could meet.

They did so now, and John stepped forward. *A ghost.* He touched her arm. *No. Real!*

"What's the matter, John?"

"Nothing," he said slowly. She looked a quarter-century younger than the last time he'd seen her. "Just… you had some flour on your arm."

His grandmother smiled. "Here now, shut the door. It's cold outside."

He turned back, surprised. Night had come, and snow fell steadily upon a sea of drifting white. Smoke rose from chimneys all down the street. Luminaria lit every driveway. Golden Christmas stars shone through tinsel on every telephone pole.

Numbly, he shut the door on the winter night.

"All day you've wanted to open presents, and now you're stalling! We have to eat if we want the strength to tackle that mountain beneath the tree." Grandma bustled off to the kitchen. "Your place is all ready," she called over her shoulder. "You can sit next to your Grandpa. And remember, don't give Sandy any turkey!"

Mouth working silently, John stepped into the living room.

Sandy, his dog, dead twenty years, lifted her head from its place of rest beneath the piano bench and eyed him drowsily before flopping back down again. On that bench sat his mother, twenty-five years younger, playing "O Holy Night"—fingers nimble, no arthritis. On a nearby couch his father talked with Great-Uncle Tom, who'd died of heart failure when John was 21. And listening quietly from the overstuffed armchair by the reading lamp—

"Grandpa," John mouthed.

The old man listened quietly to the conversations around him, saying little, but his presence filled the room like that of a benign king: John's hero of heroes, who had died of a heart attack in the February snow a week before John's tenth birthday.

Before anyone except Sandy and his grandmother noticed he was there, John stepped quickly up the stairs and raced down the hallway to the bathroom. Breathing fast and heavily, he sank to his knees by the eagle-clawed tub.

It was the carpet that brought him back to himself—the fuzzy yellow strands, so familiar, that he ran through his clutching fingers.

Gingerly, he got to his feet. Ever so slowly the world stopped spinning. He looked in the bathroom mirror.

The face of a nine-year-old boy met his gaze.

He looked down at his hands. Big, worn, and glazed with years of work and living, he turned his palms up, then let them fall limply to his sides.

Through all his tumbling thoughts, one broke out louder than the rest. *Dinner's waiting*, it reminded him.

Dinner's waiting.

Five minutes later, John stepped down the stairs and joined his family at the table.

It was a table surrounded by a dozen faces, its surface warm and breathing with the good smells he'd forgotten or half-forgotten, and he ate like he never had as a real child—two helpings, then two slices of pie washed down with milk and orange pop. He sat on the wooden bench pulled in from the kitchen, wedged between his grandparents, his dog beneath his feet, his young parents laughing about distant memories still recent to them, to everyone except him, and soon all his panic and disorientation fell away, lulled to sleep by his grandfather's beloved voice and the smell of his great aunt's green bean casserole. The frosted windowpanes fogged with steam. Uncles laughed. Cousins argued. And he, now the youngest again, thought of what he should say—all the things he'd wanted to tell these people which had come to mind far, far too late; all the questions that, through the years, he'd wanted to ask yet hadn't...What had they *been?*

He remained silent. But in the ebb and flow of the meal John was aware, from time to time, of his grandfather's gaze upon him.

After dinner, it was back to the living room and the Christmas tree, all white tinsel and red bulbs, angel decorations and gold lights. And presents piled beneath it. And he, the youngest, to hand them out.

He did, enjoying the old job like no other.

Then, sitting in a giant circle, everyone took turns opening them. For John that meant clothes offset by a baseball glove and a fossil kit, a new pencil case for school and half a dozen *Star Wars* figures.

I still have these somewhere, he thought. *Packed away, battle-damaged, accessories lost. And the baseball glove—stolen in sixth grade by Bert Winger!*

After all the presents had been opened and a second round of desserts eaten, cousins began to trickle off home and the house took on a drowsy feel. His parents spoke softly with Grandma and a few remaining uncles and aunts in the living room. Sandy, a bow on her head, slept once again beneath the piano bench. And John, forgotten for the moment, stole out to the back porch, dark but for the lights shining through the kitchen windows, and took a deep breath of cold winter air.

"Hi, Grandpa," he said.

"Hello yourself!" The old man, tall even when sitting, waved him over to the wicker chair beside him. His breath, raspy from the Black Lung that eventually killed him, sawed through the silence of the night in a quiet rhythm. They sat side by side for a long time, there in his grandfather's favorite place, until Grandpa finally spoke again.

"Tell me, John, what's on your mind?"

John turned to look at him. The old man gazed back intently.

"I…" He stopped, started again, fell silent.

"Let me help," his grandfather continued. "All day you've been different. Your mannerisms, your smile, even your appetite!" He chuckled at John's expression. "Surprised I noticed?"

"No," John said immediately. "You always saw everything."

"*Saw.* Past-tense." His grandfather nodded. "There's the rub. Eyes, John. A famous dead writer once said eyes are windows to the soul. And your eyes? They, too, are different this evening."

John looked out into the darkened back yard, clear moonlight shining down on a perfect blanket of glittering snow. In the middle of the yard he could just make out the shadow of the old maple tree that lightning had struck down when he was nineteen.

"Grandpa, can I ask you something?"

"You know you can."

John licked his lips. "What if I told you that a man, thirty-five years old, was cleaning up his grandparents' former home and deciding whether or not to sell it. And that after taking a walk around the block to clear his head, his grandmother, who… who…" He cast a sideways glance at his grandfather. The old man looked back at him steadily.

"…who was no longer around, *answered the door.* And that he walked out of a June afternoon in 2008 and into a winter evening in—"

"1983," Grandpa finished, leaning forward and smiling faintly. "And what if I told you that when a certain old man looked at his nine year-old grandson a quarter-hour to midnight on Christmas Night, 1983, he saw a thirty-five year-old man looking back at him from behind his face?"

John swallowed. "I'd say he was a very perceptive old man whose grandson still loves him very much."

Another long silence, save for the old man's breathing and a slight rocking of the chairs. Then:

"Grandpa, why am I here?"

The old man coughed, a great racking cough that shook his body. John winced.

"I'm fine," said his grandfather. "But I don't have all the answers. Why am *I* here? Either of us? Brought together out of time. No, no answers."

John sighed.

"But if I had to *guess?*"

Now it was John's turn to lean forward.

"I'd guess you're here to say goodbye."

The breath kicked out of John's body. "*No.*"

His grandfather nodded. "John, I've always said I want to live to see you graduate high school. From the look in your eyes tonight, that doesn't—*didn't* —work out." He paused. "There were so many things I could have told you during those later years," he said. "So much advice, some of it even good."

He smiled, and John, after an unsteady moment, did likewise.

Grandpa glanced at the white face of his gold watch. "Ten minutes to midnight," he mused. "So I have to choose my advice carefully. Something tells me that at midnight, this gift will have run its course. So here."

He cleared his throat and stood up. He opened the screen door. Together they walked around to the front sidewalk, where they could take in the whole panorama of the house.

"When I was in college, working nights in the mines and taking classes by day, I took an acting course. Did you know that?"

John shook his head.

"Well, I wasn't any good. Instead, happily, a teacher's life for me."

"And me," John added.

Grandpa nodded approvingly. "Well, in this acting class we learned that an actor can only return for so many bows, no matter how successful the show. I think this is my last bow to you, John. And you, in the audience, must likewise go home, leave the theater, and continue on. There's nothing more depressing than an empty theater, seats folded, lights up, then off, and all the people who gave it life gone elsewhere."

A strong hand squeezed John's shoulder. He grabbed it, and the house full of warmth and light blurred until he wiped his eyes.

"Now Christmas is almost over, and I want to give you one final gift," said Grandpa. "I want you to go back in, take a good look around, give everyone a hug, and sneak Sandy a piece of turkey. And when you do, tell each of them you love them. I'd trade almost anything to go back and do that to the people I loved. And you can."

"And *then*?"

"Then go up to your bedroom, slide under the quilt your grandmother made you, and go to sleep. And, sleeping, dream of all the good things the future will bring. Then, when you wake at dawn, leave this house and never come back."

John took one final look at the half-dozen cars in the driveway, at the orange Christmas candles in each window, at the well-lit living room from which muffled laughter touched the otherwise silent night. Then together, hand in hand, John and his grandfather walked up the steps to the front door and into the waiting warmth.

* * *

And in another year, a bright, sunny June morning, John woke on the bare floor of his old room, oddly refreshed. Quickly he descended the stairs, shut the front door behind him, and locked it. He pulled his car out of the weed-choked driveway, and, humming, clicked the gear into drive.

Looking back at the house through his rearview mirror, he thought he caught a glimpse of someone—*two* people—waving from the open front doorway.

He blinked and looked again. Now the door was shut, just as he'd left it.

Still humming, he drove toward home.

The Character

Every day Wilfred Colson sat at a corner table in the café area of the bookstore, and every day he observed the people who sat around him. At first, head to his computer, he tried to block them out. They were an enormous distraction, especially the women with their occasional high-pitched giggles and the old men who felt the need to scream into the cell phones their children had bought them. But then, slowly, he came around. They were *characters* in their way, and hadn't Dickens mastered his art of dialect and description by staring out at the London streets while working as a clerk in a lawyer's office?

So he began paying attention. Every so often, taking a break from his newest story or novel, he would allow the outside world fully in. The results were extraordinary—as were the regulars who arrived at their tables with clockwork routine: the wild-haired old man who wore the same blue shirt every day, grimaced at anyone who looked at him, and nursed the same cup of tepid coffee for two hours without once reaching for a book or magazine; the "Doll Ladies," who met every third Thursday of the month, with their gastrointestinal complaints, creepy three-foot-tall dolls, disturbingly detailed back stories for the "babies," and brightly-colored muumuus; and, of course, the towering giant who ate five doughnuts with colored sprinkles, told startled strangers about his brother's unexpected murder, then invariably exited through the fire escape, setting off all the alarms in the building.

There were others, too. People passing through with their quirks, eccentricities, and foibles. These he never saw more than once or twice, but there was always *someone* interesting and worthy of a couple pages of notes. And before he knew it, they began to enter into his short stories fully-formed. Colson had turned a nuisance into art and was suitably pleased with himself. Soon he began a series of stories based entirely upon people he observed in the café. The project promised to be an interesting character study that, Colson hoped, might end up as something of a post-modern *Winesburg, Ohio.*

He first noticed the new guy several months after starting the collection. Unusually diminutive and tiny (no more than four-feet, ten inches tall), unusually expressive (he smiled at virtually everyone in sight, though never engaged anyone beyond that), and also possessing the uncanny ability to sense when someone was staring at him, the "Little Fellow" (as Colson named him) quickly became a regular.

This made Colson's observations difficult but entertaining. He liked a challenge, and the struggle to take notes on the man while sparring with his apparent sixth sense enlivened more than a few dull days.

Everything was going fine until three weeks after the Little Fellow first caught his attention. Colson, hard at work and in "The Zone," reached for his cooling cup of Chai and touched, instead, a clammy, thin-fingered hand.

Startled, he looked up. The Little Fellow stood just inches away, smiling at him. "Hello," the man said, and sat down at Colson's table.

Bemused, Colson cleared his throat. "Yes, hello there. May I ask what you're doing?"

"I could ask you the same question, Mr. Colson."

He blinked. "How do you know my name?"

"I'm a reader, Mr. Colson. Along with the works of many other authors, I also read *yours*. Because of that, I know what you look like and I know you're local. Makes sense."

Colson nodded. "Yes, it does." He didn't like meeting fans in informal settings. They took up too much of his time, and disentangling himself from their questions and requests was distracting and tiring. He hoped he could shoo the man away quickly by being as terse as possible.

He opened his mouth to say something curt, but the Little Fellow interrupted. "You've been watching me, Mr. Colson." He wagged a thin finger in mock admonition. "Now don't try and deny it!"

Colson thought fast. Perhaps honesty would be best. It wouldn't do to have a short story appear with the Little Fellow in it (such as the one he was writing now), then have to deal with a resentful source of inspiration after the fact. He would turn on the charm and see if that worked.

"Yes," he said, "I have to admit you've got me there, Mr…"

"Bagby. Burt Bagby."

(*Better than Little Fellow,* Colson thought.)

"Ah. Mr. Bagby."

"Ever heard of me?"

Colson shook his head. "Sorry."

Bagby looked hurt. "I've been published in *Merry Times, Hard Rain,* and *Lost Stars.* I write stories too, you see."

"Oh! Well, congratulations. You see, Mr.… um…"

"*Bag*by," said the little man, smiling again.

"Mr. Bagby. Yes. You see, I've recently started using my surroundings as inspiration. Particularly, ah, *people* in my surroundings."

"Hey, like Dickens!"

Colson was surprised and somewhat pleased. "Yes, exactly like Dickens. And I'm afraid, Mr. Bagby, that you caught my eye. I'm sorry if this is unacceptable. If so, I can tear up the story I've started, and—"

Bagby gripped his arm. "Not on your life!" he said, mouth suddenly tight, eyes wide and gleaming. Perhaps feeling he had overstepped, he released Colson's sleeve, leaned back, and mopped his brow. "How fortuitous. How positively lovely. I'm honored, Mr. Colson."

Colson smoothed his sleeve. "Well, I thank you, Mr. Bagby. I'm a bit embarrassed to be *caught* like this, but you have good eyes. And I appreciate your understanding."

"A character in one of your stories! Wonderful."

"Yes, indeed. A minor character, but a character nonetheless. Well, I must be going." The whole tenor of his work day had been thrown off. Colson was finished for the afternoon.

* * *

And that, he thought, was that.

Except it wasn't.

In the weeks that followed, little Burt Bagby seemed to be everywhere, at all times. At Starbucks. At Wash & Go. At Giant Eagle. And at the bookstore, of course. Always at the bookstore.

It took Colson some time to realize what was happening. When he did, he was more annoyed than worried. Finally, a month later, during a break in his writing at the bookstore café, Colson looked up, and there was Bagby again. It was too much. This latest appearance had toppled the stack.

Colson caught Bagby's eye and motioned to him. Smile wide as always, Bagby jumped up and scampered over.

"Look here," Colson said, tapping the table top with a bony index finger. "You've got to stop this. It isn't proper and it isn't dignified. You say you admire my work? Then do it and me the favor of allowing me to continue it. I can't write when I'm distracted, and you, Mr. Bagby, are becoming a distraction."

Obviously wounded, Mr. Bagby looked around the café. "This is a public place, Mr. Colson," he said. "We live in the same town. We go out in public. It's bound to happen, that we see each other."

"Not eleven times in two weeks!"

"Hmm! Well, perhaps you've got me there. But you have to admit, all this makes for an interesting character, doesn't it? Perhaps a somewhat *important* character?"

Before Colson could get over his shock, Bagby rose to his feet, tipped his hat, and sauntered off.

And Colson couldn't be sure, but the one time Bagby looked back, he thought he caught a wink.

* * *

Two months passed. In December, in the middle of the night, Colson woke from a fretful sleep, crossed to his window, scraped away the frost, and blinked out at the silver nightscape.

Burt Bagby, bald head reflecting moonlight, was kneeling by Colson's car, letting the air out of his tires.

Colson couldn't believe it. He'd seen less of Bagby over the previous few weeks and figured his pep talk had served its purpose.

He threw open the window. "Hey, there! You! Bagby! I'm coming down! I'm calling the police!"

"Good! Wonderful!" Bagby called back. "Aren't I *eccentric*, though? Aren't I *unpredictable*?"

"No! Now clear off!"

Without another word, Bagby scampered away.

* * *

After that, Colson didn't see Bagby for close to three months. He hadn't bothered calling the police on him; Colson hated distractions, and since the vandalism went unrepeated, he decided to let the matter drop.

But the incident had bothered him; his whole sense of peaceful routine had been compromised, and his writing had suffered as a result. Bagby could be *any*where, doing *any*thing, at *any time.* His absence, if anything, made Colson more disconcerted than his constant appearances. Because of that, Colson's writing had fallen behind schedule for the first time in nearly fifteen years, the quality had likely suffered too, and that simply wouldn't do.

Happily, he had chosen a solution, should the day come when Mr. Burt Bagby dared show his face again.

That day came late in March, when Colson, sitting at his usual table, swatting away at his slacks in the bookstore after dumping some caramel latte on them, looked up to find Bagby's pallid, lightly sweating face just inches from his own.

"Hello there, old chum! Miss me?" Bagby cried.

"Ack!" Colson choked, slopping more latte on himself.

Bagby pulled up a chair. "How've you been?" he asked. "Lots of good ideas? Lots of *character* development?" He pantomimed elbowing Colson in the ribs. "I thought I'd give you some uninterrupted time to think about me, but I figured I'd given you long enough. Now I'm back!"

A cold fury awoke in Colson. The tips of his fingers turned to ice. A vein pumped alarmingly in his temple.

"Mr. Bagby," he said in a low voice—flat, calm, and dangerous. "You are an annoyance, Mr. Bagby. A burr in my sock, quickly removed and just as quickly forgotten. Additionally you strike me as somewhat pitiful—*pathetic* might be a better adjective. I assume you are single and are likely to remain so not by choice, but by circumstance. You are also a failure. A failure as a writer, and, by proxy, a failure as a person; a late-middle aged sycophant. And I hate to break this to you, Mr. Bagby, but I don't write about pathetic, annoying, sycophantic failures. You will *never* be a character in any work of mine. Not even a minor one. The story I was writing didn't pan out with you in it... because, simply, you're a *bore*."

Mr. Bagby's face lost a great deal of color during Colson's controlled explosion. Surprisingly, he regained it fairly quickly.

"I see," he said. "Well, that leaves me just one option, then. Since *you* won't write about *me*, *I* will have to write about *you*.

Because you are, as I'm sure most of your millions of readers would readily confirm, an 'interesting character,' Mr. Colson."

Colson chuckled. "By all means! If it makes you happy, turn me into a character for one of your stories. Publish it in one of your little 'zines. Good luck to you! Now *goodbye.*"

Bagby shook his head. "I wasn't talking about fiction, Mr. Colson. No, I thought I'd try my hand at something else. A memoir, perhaps."

Colson snorted. "Nonsense. Who would want to read what *you* have to say about *me?*"

"Oh, I think a great many people will," Bagby said, smiling faintly. "Many, many people indeed."

And without so much as another word between them, Bagby reached out and cut Colson's throat.

BRADBURY
MOBY DICK
DANDELION WINE
THE ODYSSEY
BEOWULF

The Leasehold of His Days

The ultrasound showed it and there could be no doubt. His wife was pregnant. Two years of trying and it had finally happened.

Jason Emery walked out of the hospital in a startled daze, numbed by a strange sense of unreality.

"Whatcha thinking?" asked Susan.

"I… I don't really know."

"That's a first."

He stopped walking. So did Susan.

"My mind's a rush," he said. "It doesn't know what to focus on. What… how…" He paused, breathing heavily. "What does being a father *mean*? Most of all. In one simple sentence. I need something to hold on to, or I'm never going to know how to feel or what to do. I've wanted this so long, but now…"

Susan laughed and continued walking. He fell in step beside her. "I don't think there *is* one simple sentence that sums up what it means to be a parent. If there was, life would be simpler to understand." She pinched his arm. "You're thinking too much. That's the problem. Parenting isn't just in the head—it's in the glands, too."

"Maybe," he said.

* * *

Was it true?

Late that night he sat in his study, surrounded by his books. They were a constant source of comfort and always had been, even back in college when he'd owned only a couple of dozen battered paperbacks. Now he was a school librarian, and surrounding himself with the subjects of his love kept him grounded and safe. So when he wanted to think, when he was lost, this, his *own* library, was where he went. Answers, if they were to come, came to him here.

He scanned the shelves. *The Great Gatsby*, *The Scarlet Letter*, *Dandelion Wine*, *Adventures of Huckleberry Finn*, *The Canterbury Tales*, *In Our Time*…

More: *The Collected Poems of Dylan Thomas*, *The Secret Histories*, *Wind in the Willows*, *Memoirs of Ulysses S. Grant*, *Idylls of the King*, *The Iliad*, *Beowulf*…

He stopped, pulled *Beowulf* from the shelf, opened to a random page, and read:

…Beowulf was foiled
of a glorious victory. The glittering sword,
infallible before that day,
failed when he unsheathed it, as it never should have.
For the son of Ecgtheow, it was no easy thing
to have to give ground like that and go
unwillingly to inhabit another home
in a place beyond; so every man must yield
the leasehold of his days.

Jason sighed.

At the beginning of every year he started the first day of school with a little speech to the classes visiting the library. "Remember," he told them, "the greatest thing about writing is that it lets you communicate with someone from another time, another place. When you open *The Odyssey*, Homer speaks to you across the seas and across the millennia. The Greeks roar through his blind lines. You read, he breathes. You turn a page, his voice is carried on its whisper."

He looked down at his battered copy of *Beowulf*, written by an unknown poet 1300 years before.

"But he *is* known," Jason murmured. "Each line is a thought, each stanza a bellow across time. That nameless scop will never die."

On certain rare occasions, always late at night, a despair, also nameless, would wake him from sleep, toss and turn his thoughts, and spin him downstairs to sit beneath the neon kitchen light for long hours before exhaustion drove him back to bed. He didn't think of such times often, but he did now.

And, thinking, Jason realized the root of his despair was the certain, heartbreaking realization that *he* would not be among those who spoke across time. He tended books but did not create them. His own writing had never amounted to anything. When he died, his voice would be silenced forever.

His hands went cold. A shiver of incredible sadness etched his spine. He gasped, the backs of his beloved books spinning. *Beowulf* fell from his hands to the carpet, pages crumpling, spine splaying wide. He cried out—

Then fell silent.

Only the pounding of his heart, a deep metronome of seconds, thumped in the darkened house. Upstairs, his wife continued sleeping. No dogs barked outside.

His frantic eyes had caused his quiet, for they had alighted upon the open page of the broken book. With a mind of their own, they had read the words of Beowulf's dying moment. With more than his mind, he understood them:

Now is the time when I would have wanted
to bestow this armour on my own son,
had it been my fortune to have fathered an heir
and live on in his flesh…

And Jason suddenly remembered why he was here, what had brought him down to his books in the middle of the night, why his racing mind had been unable to sleep.

His heartbeat slowed.

Suddenly very tired, he replaced *Beowulf* carefully on its shelf, rested his hand on it for a long moment, then went back upstairs.

At the top of the landing he paused, brought up short by a photograph hooked on the wall. Young eyes gazed out at him from across the years—his own. And his small, young hand held that of another—his father, dead three years.

Jason took a deep breath. The day of that photo had been a fine one. He and his dad had gone fishing, and he'd caught a five-inch trout; barely a minnow, but his first, and his father had made him feel like he'd single-handedly landed Moby Dick.

He looked at the small, young hand, tightly clutching his father's reassuringly large one, then turned away. He held out his hand and examined it closely in the moonlight—the little hairs, the worn ridges. His eyes widened, as if seeing it, *really* seeing it, for the first time.

Two minutes later, back in bed, he fell instantly asleep.

* * *

The next morning Jason tripped lightly down the hall and poured himself a cup of coffee.

"You slept in!" Susan exclaimed, spreading grape jam on a piece of toast.

"It was a topsy-turvy night."

"Coffee?"

"You bet." He surveyed the kitchen and smiled, then picked up the newspaper and scanned the headlines.

"You're awfully chipper this morning," she said. "After all that stress yesterday, I'm surprised."

"Some friends helped me find the answers I was looking for."

"No more crises about the nature of fatherhood?"

"None."

Susan set down her piece of toast. She gave Jason a long, appraising look.

"You have good friends," she said.

Jason smiled. "It's a beautiful day. I'm going for a walk. Wanna come?"

On their way out the door Jason paused by a small mirror. He looked at himself closely.

"Hi, Dad," he said quietly. "It's good to see you."

EXIT
5,000 CUTS
HAIRCUTS CUTS! CUTS!
CUTS! KUTS!
©2012

A Quick Break

Brian Lumley knew how important it was to get away from the books for a few hours every week or so. Penn State, for all its possible avenues of growth, could become a stifling place, especially with final exams approaching. But without money, car, or time, even getting out for a haircut and a cup of coffee was difficult—and the best he could do.

He shook rain from his coat as he pushed open the glass doors to the Nittany Mall. Just inside, he encountered a contest in full swing.

SHOW YOUR PATRIOTISM FOR A CHANCE TO WIN BIG! a giant banner read. Beneath it, a least a hundred people had surrounded a particleboard stage by the big fountain. On it, above a line of perhaps two dozen other hopefuls, a pimply teen with braces and corn-shuck hair stood awkwardly, belting out the national anthem for all she was worth.

Brian winced as she veered off key, stumbled, resumed, then finished to a smattering of applause. He ducked into Holiday Haircuts, signed in, and took a seat. Flipping through a well-thumbed *Newsweek*, he tried to read, but found himself distracted as more contestants took their turns. The din of the noise coupled with the neon lights of the salon left him feeling slightly anxious.

"Hello there."

He looked up.

A plump, smiling old lady took a seat. Brian noticed that although the waiting area was empty, she'd chosen the seat directly beside him. He could smell her perfume—lilacs—and see a tiny smudge of makeup caked in the crease between her ear and face, just beneath the closely-permed white hair.

"Goodness, but I'm glad to see it isn't crowded. I didn't even have an appointment!"

He smiled. "Oh, you don't need one here. They're never very busy this early in the morning."

"That's good to know. Thank heavens for that!"

Brian liked the look of her. She seemed down-home, agreeable, and relaxed… quite different from most of the people he knew on campus. It felt good to get away for a quick break, even if it *was* for a mundane reason.

"You have a busy day planned?" he ventured.

"Oh, yes. Yes, indeed! I'm here visiting my son, and I can't be late."

"You're from out of town?"

She nodded. "Pittsburgh. But while I was driving up, I happened to look in the mirror, and my *land*, what a sight! I thought, 'You can't be seeing your son like *that*, can you?' And I knew the answer was no. So I stopped off here. I still have an hour to spare before I'm expected."

Brian nodded. Behind him, out in the mall, a small child wailed about "the land of the free" so shrilly the sound system gave off an earsplitting shriek of reverb. He winced.

"Well, I hope you have a good day together," he said, determined to drown out the noise. "Does your son live in State College? Or Bellefonte, maybe?"

The old lady looked at him with eyes suddenly wide and glassy. "Oh, no, no, I'm off to Blairsville to see a psychic! Just five miles down the road."

"Hmm?" He furrowed his brow. "I don't understand. Didn't you say you were going to visit your son?"

"Oh, yes, dear!" she exclaimed, grasping his wrist in a firm, clammy grip, giving it a hard squeeze, then releasing it. "My son is dead, you see. They found his body next to his car on Route 26 three years ago. Not a drop of blood left in it."

Brian blinked rapidly. Finally, he cleared his throat.

"I'm… I'm sorry," he said lamely. His lips worked silently a bit longer before he added, "Um… what are you going to ask him? The psychic, I mean. Or, you know, your son *through* the psychic. Or… or whatever."

"Oh, that's simple!" The woman threw back her head and cackled. "I'm going to ask what happened to his head! They never found it!"

"I see." Brian's vision blurred.

The lights, the singing, the perfume, the laughter…

"Well, ma'am, I think I'm going to go out and watch the contest while I wait," he announced as brightly as he could. "I love the national anthem."

"Oh, good idea!" She squeezed his wrist again, pumping it hard with her damp, cool palm. "Isn't that precious?"

Brian felt nauseated as he staggered out into the mall.

On stage, a fat man with a tobacco-stained beard and jean overalls was belting out the part about the "dawn's early light."

Brian walked quickly back to the glass doors and pushed through them, stepping out into the cold, wet day again. He hoped the bus to campus would come early. He needed to get back there, he really did. He no longer wanted a haircut. He no longer wanted to get away.

"A break," he muttered, pacing back and forth in the rain, letting the cold drops numb his skin. "It was just a quick break."

DOGGIE!

Dead End

Cutting his parents' lawn just wasn't enough anymore. Summer wouldn't last forever and James needed more money. He wanted that iPhone, *had to have* that iPhone, and time was ticking by.

Taking his incentive from Harry Larkin, an older boy who always seemed to be mowing a lawn somewhere in the neighborhood, he set to work. After several hours with paste, pencil, and marker he headed out to post two dozen signs around the neighborhood. They read:

Lawn need mowed??
Leaves need raked??
Dog need sat??
CALL JAMES BROCK!
1-814-555-8927
109 Sycamore
CHEAP RATES!!

That done, James sat back and waited for the money to roll in.

He waited a long time. Rain streaked the signs. Wind blew some of them away. No one called, no one came by.

"Why?" he asked his mother.

"Maybe Harry Larkin's got the market cornered," she answered.

"Why?" he asked his father.

"The economy," the old man answered, but didn't elaborate.

Then, just when everything seemed positively hopeless, Mrs. Wentworth knocked on the door.

The old lady was a piece of work. James had never spoken two words to her before. She chased children off her property on Halloween and scowled at them from her living room window while they waited for the bus. She walked around the block every evening, humming a strange tune, but never said hello to anyone and grumbled when they made any overture. Once a year, on Christmas Eve, she attended church, but never stayed for the reception afterward.

So James was amazed to find her standing there, clutching one of his faded signs in a skeletal, blue-veined hand.

"You sit dogs?" she demanded abruptly. "The sign says you sit dogs."

"Er," James replied.

"You an idiot, boy? I don't have the time of day for idiots." She pursed her lips.

"Uh... that is, no ma'am. And yeah, I sit dogs." He'd added that job to his signs as an afterthought. To the best of his knowledge, Harry Larkin didn't sit dogs. Not that James knew much about how to do it himself.

"Well, I need my dog taken care of. His name's Riley, and he's a sweet fellow. Kinda big. No trouble, though. He's too old for trouble. What do you charge?"

"Ten dollars a day," he said promptly, rattling off his spiel. "That gets you two feedings and two walks, plus all messes cleaned up. Should there be any. And it's two dollars a day extra if I have to give him any medicine."

The old woman signed impatiently. "Highway robbery. I'll give you eight. No walks needed. Riley's too old. And no medicine, either. Deal?" She stuck out her hand.

James shook it. Her hand was cold and dry. Later, he brushed some hair from his eyes and happened to smell the fingers that had touched hers. They stank like something gone rotten, covered over with talc.

"You begin tomorrow morning," she said, clearly ready to be on her way. "Eight. Then again at four. The key is under the mat. The food is on the counter. I'll pay you when I get back from my sister's next Sunday. She's got arthritis real bad, but it's a pain for both of us, let me tell you."

And then she was gone.

James stood in the doorway blinking.

"Mom!" he shouted. "Mom, I've got a job!"

* * *

He was curious about Mrs. Wentworth's house. Entering it was like entering enemy territory, except that suddenly it was OK, he was allowed, and that made it even stranger.

But what James found left him disappointed: a slightly musty, perfume-laden home filled with faded photographs, a broken record player, old prayer books, frilly curtains, and the kind of precious knick-knacks the five-and-dime sold at the back of the store for 75% off. It was exactly like Great-Aunt Irene's house: a place that bored him to tears the three times a year his parents forced him to go there.

James sighed. Where was Riley?

He remembered the dog vaguely: a brown Great Dane, paws the size of a bear's, with lanky strides and a droopy muzzle. He hadn't seen it outside in a long time. Too old, he supposed, like Mrs. Wentworth had said.

He sneezed. Really, he'd never been in a place so covered in perfume. Like funeral flowers, he thought fleetingly. The old lady must drench herself in it. And everything she owned.

Riley. He walked slowly through the living room and back into the foyer, then started down the hall.

James hated empty houses. He didn't like being alone, didn't like it when his parents went to dinner or parties or the movies and wouldn't let him come. Didn't like the way every sound amplified, every piece of furniture loomed when only he was there. Didn't like the pregnant, waiting darkness as he moved from room to room, or the cold, impersonal light when he flicked the switches on.

He had never been alone in a stranger's home before. Somehow that was much worse. And maybe it was the strangeness of the place, sure, but there was something else he couldn't quite put his finger on… a hostile, bleak feeling. Later, when he was older, he would recognize it for what it was: the knowledge that he had entered a part of the world that didn't know him, that he hadn't touched and which didn't need his presence, that didn't care if he lived or died.

Moving down the hallway, steps slow and unsteady, he marveled as the heady, stifling air grew denser and more saturated. Roses and lilies, wild gardenias. His stomach lurched. He swallowed. Lilac. Tulips and chrysanthemums…

Where was Riley?

"Here, boy," he called in the thick stillness. No sound of the dog. James entered the kitchen and caught a whiff of something else, something buried beneath the flowers. It made him remember shaking hands with Mrs. Wentworth, of the bad smell on her fingers.

He flicked on the light switch. The smell, the stench, gained identity.

Riley lay in a huge wicker basket. Both it and the dog were covered with flies. They streamed over the body, rose disturbed and buzzing to resettle, and beneath them James caught sight of things white and wriggling, things he'd only seen before on dead birds and rabbits left on hot, blacktopped roads. Everything about the basket and the body seemed in motion—two things made one by a seething, boiling sea.

As he ran from the house, sleeve over his mouth, eyes streaming, he thought, *I hate the cold light in empty houses. Hate it, hate it, hate it…*

Then he was home, back where he belonged, in a part of the world where people lived who cared about him, where things made sense, where he felt safe.

But not as safe as he once had been.

* * *

A week passed. Mrs. Wentworth hadn't left a number where she could be reached and didn't call. James' father buried the dog in Mrs. Wentworth's side yard and returned home sweaty and pale. His mother helped clean out the kitchen.

Both his parents spoke words of comfort to James, trying to shrug off what had happened, to joke about it, to let him know *it wasn't his fault.*

Well, no kidding, he thought.

But at night they talked, and James, sitting half-way down on the stairs, heard.

"That dog had been dead for weeks," his father said, folding the newspaper.

"James mustn't see her again," his mother replied over the sound of Johnny Carson. "When she comes over, I'll talk to her."

But Mrs. Wentworth didn't come over.

* * *

"*What did you do with Riley?*"

The words were a shriek, barely language.

"I… I…," said James.

He'd been expecting Brooke Newcomb to call with help on his math homework. Instead, it was Mrs. Wentworth.

"You *buried* him?"

"I… yes!" he blurted. "Yes, he was *dead.* He was… there were flies, and—"

"Well of *course* he was dead, but *you buried him*?"

James held the phone, still and silent, not daring to suck air.

"That means you didn't *feed* him. All week *without food*!" Mrs. Wentworth was breathing heavily. Then, seeming to calm herself, she took one big, deep breath and said, more evenly, "Well, I think you can see why I won't be paying you, young man."

And with that, she hung up.

* * *

James took the long way around the block for weeks, all to avoid passing Mrs. Wentworth's house on foot. He didn't mind, except that the longer walks gave him more time to think. Sometimes, he discovered, thinking too much wasn't a good thing.

For instance, he often found himself thinking about the newly-dug hole in Mrs. Wentworth's side yard—the hole his father had dug and filled, and which was now empty again, dirt piled up alongside it. He could see it every time the bus passed her house to and from school.

And invariably, when he thought of that, he also thought of his father's comment after he'd told him about Mrs. Wentworth's phone call. His father was a man of few words. But when he spoke, James usually listened.

"I suppose," his father had told him, handing him a new iPhone, "that you'd best take down those signs. That business venture of yours was kind of a dead end, don't you think?"

Yes, he did, but he didn't want to think *too* much. Not about that. No, he didn't want that at all.

And looking at his new iPhone, a gateway to the homes of a billion strangers, James suddenly felt as though he were holding a part of the world that didn't know him, that he hadn't touched and which didn't need his presence, that didn't care if he lived or died.

Graduation Day

It was 1996, it was May, it was a Friday, and evening was already coming on. As always, Patrick Hughes wanted to go out. His mother had given him the Corolla, the loan good until his eleven o'clock curfew, so after dinner he escaped into the fading sunlight and warm twilight air, buckled himself in, and had already dialed the first number on his new cell phone before even clearing the driveway.

He called Bill Plourde, his best friend, as he headed, without really thinking, toward the Columbia Mall.

No answer.

Strange. He'd said he would be around. Well…

Charlie Karavlan, then. Charlie was always up for anything. And wherever he was, others were too.

"Charlie?"

"Sorry, Pat," said Charlie's father. "He's away for the weekend."

"What? Really?" Charlie hadn't mentioned that in school.

"Sorry," Mr. Karavlan repeated, and hung up.

Shaking his head, Patrick dialed his girlfriend, Lisa. The phone rang ten times. He frowned, hung up, dialed again. Nothing. Not even her voice mail. Same with her home number… it just rang and rang, no answering machine message, nothing.

Two stoplights from the mall, he abruptly took a right turn, cut through the neighborhood of Thunder Hill, and continued calling numbers, now systematically going down the list of his friends. Dave Turnbull? No answer. Brian Sheets? Out. Rich York?

Someone strange answered the phone when he called Rich's home number.

"Who?" It sounded like an old lady. Was his grandmother visiting?

"Rich. Rich York. This is his number."

"I don't know no Rich York."

He paused. Maybe the old lady was senile.

"Are you visiting family?" he asked. "Is this the York house?"

Click.

Maybe he'd misdialed. But no, he was pulling the numbers from his contact list. The dialing was automated.

With a sign of relief he pulled into Lisa's driveway. He honked the horn. No one came out.

"Jesus. *Someone* has to be home. Mrs. Horowitz never leaves the damned house."

He got out of the car and slammed the door. The night—*full* night now—was dark, a deep ebony. No streetlamps, and Lisa's front door lamps weren't lit. Patrick felt the hair on the back of his neck and rubbed away a shiver. He rang the doorbell.

Flower, Lisa's German Shepherd, didn't bark on the other side. She *always* barked.

No lights came on.

He peered in the garage windows, cupping his hands to ward off reflections.

No cars.

"What the *hell* is going on?" His voice sounded weak and thin in the thick, late-spring air.

Ten miles away and fifteen minutes later, he pulled into VIPs, his favorite pool hall. Every other Friday night for three years he'd gone there, usually with half a dozen friends, to play eight-ball, smoke, cuss, and eat frozen candy bars from the freezer behind the counter, fifty cents each, before turning to the old arcade games along the far wall, then heading out to the Double-T Diner for late-night dinner.

He pushed open the broken glass door and entered fast, scanning the cool darkness, the whispering fans, the muted yellow lights over each threadbare table.

It was too quiet. A couple of old men played billiards nearby, but the rest of the tables were clear and empty, and so were the arcade stools.

"Evening," said the attendant behind the counter—an old man missing his top front teeth. "How many hours you want?"

Patrick took another look around.

"Kind of dead tonight, huh?"

The attendant laughed dryly. "When is it ever not?"

"Last Friday there were fifty people in here. Hey, I never saw you before. Where's Carl?"

The attendant pushed his tongue through the gap in his teeth and whistled. "Son, you been drinkin'?"

"No."

"Then you'd know I own this place. And I can't remember seeing you before in all my days."

Patrick lit a cigarette with a trembling match.

"No smoking, kiddo."

"What?"

"Get gone. You make me nervous."

He didn't want to go anywhere else. In just an hour and a half the night had taken a bad turn, a surreal tinge, and all he wanted now was for it to end. But he couldn't just go home. Not on this night. And he needed to see one more place...

Patrick pulled into the parking lot of the Double-T Diner and was immensely reassured by the bright lights, the busy parking lot, the other kids milling around outside... it was all familiar. It was all *right.*

But he didn't know anyone. He always knew at least a handful of the kids who milled around out front or talked loudly at the tables, sucking up milkshakes through straws and picking at limp fries. And there was always, *always* someone he could sit with, a table he could join.

Not this time. Not now.

And he realized, with a cold shock, that he didn't belong here, that he needed to find another place to go. He just didn't know where.

So he went home.

When he arrived, Patrick half-expected the house to be dark, or to find a strange car parked in the driveway, or even for the whole place to be gone, only an empty lot left in its place.

But it was there, lights reassuringly on, cars in the driveway reassuringly familiar.

He let himself in, and there were his parents watching television, his dog asleep at his father's feet.

"Hey, you're home early, kiddo!" his father exclaimed. "Only ten o' clock!"

"I'm glad," said his mother. "Tomorrow's a big day."

"A bunch of people called for you," his father added. "Bill and Charlie and Lisa. Lisa was angry she couldn't get a hold of you. Isn't your phone working?"

"It was acting up," said Patrick faintly.

"So where did you *go* then, if you couldn't find your friends?" his mother asked.

"All over, but there wasn't..." He paused. "I couldn't find them tonight. Because… because of my phone. So I came home."

"Well, just as well, like your mother said." His father smiled. "In case you forgot, tomorrow afternoon you'll be a high school grad! You'd better be rested for the ceremony."

Patrick nodded, did his best to smile, and went up to bed.

"Graduation," he said to himself as he walked up the stairs. "Did they really think I could forget?"

And for long, long hours, after everyone else had gone to sleep, he thought about all the things from which he was graduating.

BELOVED FRIEND

Comfortable Silence

He was on an airplane, wearing an uncomfortable suit, book untouched on his lap, plastic cup empty on his tray, when the older woman next to him leaned over and asked, "Where from?"

He didn't roll his eyes—he was too polite—but he wanted to. He had no interest in talking, or at least engaging in idle chatter, but courtesy won the day.

"Pittsburgh," he said, then added, two moments later, "and yourself?"

"Cleveland. I'm going to my high school reunion." A chuckle. "My *fiftieth*."

"Hmm! Well, that's nice. I hope you have a good time." He eyed his book.

"I'm not so sure I will," she said, and the blandly affable smile often afforded strangers faded.

She wanted him to ask why.

"Why?" he asked.

"Well, you know, it's been so long. I haven't lived in Aurora for thirty-six years. And all my old friends…"

She didn't finish the sentence, so he simply nodded.

"It's not the old clichés that worry me," she went on. "You know… 'Oh, what if Sally Henderson's career went better than mine did? Oh, what if everyone aged better than I did?' I'm past all that. None of it matters."

"So what's worrying you?"

She shook her head. "It's silly, but what's kept me up these last few nights is just one question: what are we all going to talk about?"

"That's it?"

"Good heavens, isn't that *enough*? Think about it! Fifty years since we graduated. It was a small high school and we all knew each other. But after graduation we went our separate ways, and now we're all spread out across the country. A few of us even live abroad! It was easy to know each other and get along when we all had geography in common—the same town, the same classes and school hallways—but when you're thrust back into a room with people and that common ground is gone, what then?" She paused. "I'm Grace, by the way."

"Adam." He extended a hand. Grace took it.

"It was wonderful to know them," she said, sighing. "But I have a fear that's all it will ever be now—a past-tense relationship."

"So you didn't keep in touch with *any* of them?" Adam asked, surprised the conversation had pulled him out of himself a bit; he was interested in spite of everything. "I mean, a good friend that's lasted all the years?"

"Ah." Grace quieted, fiddling with the ice in her empty cup of water. She did this for quite some time, until Adam thought she wasn't going to respond at all. Then, quite suddenly, she said, "One of *those*."

"Yes. Is there one?"

"There was," she said. "Dorothy Price. A dear friend."

"*Was?*" he said. "I'm sorry...I don't mean to pry."

"No, no, not at all. Dorothy died three years ago. Heart attack. Quite unexpected."

"I'm sorry."

"Me too."

There was an awkward silence. Then Grace said, "That's funny. Looking back on it, you know what really defines a true friendship? One that lasts the years?"

"What?" He really wanted to know. He'd been thinking a good deal about friendship over the last few days.

"It's the *silences*. Do you know what I mean?"

Adam shook his head.

"You're still a young man," she said, "but as you get older, you'll see for yourself. A friend, a *true* friend—the kind you keep for life—is someone you can sit in the same room with for a minute, an hour, even *three*, without saying a word... and not feel uncomfortable that whole time. Not needing to fill the gaps with idle chatter. Comfortable silence. That's the test."

He thought about it for a long time. "Yes," he said finally, "I see what you mean. That makes good sense. I... I have someone like that in my life, in fact, although I never thought of it quite that way."

"Well do me a favor, Adam, if you don't mind."

He looked up. Grace was gazing at him steadily, earnestly, without blinking.

"Hang on to that person. Keep them in your life always."

"I will," he said firmly. "I promise."

* * *

Adam disembarked, stretched, got his luggage, took the shuttle from O'Hare to his rental car, and drove straight to the funeral home. Once there, he checked his watch. Two hours early.

He went inside. An attendant greeted him. Adam asked if he could have some time alone with the deceased.

"Are you a relative, sir?" the man inquired, his tone a perfect blend of somber empathy and professional detachment.

"A friend," he said simply. "A good friend."

The man smiled understandingly—Adam was grateful for that smile; it seemed more real than the tone—and invited him into a small anteroom.

The coffin, closed, gleamed in the half-light, a sideways monolith of polished brass. Far different from the elderly man whose remains it contained: Adam's dear old friend, a professor from long ago whose lessons spanned all the years. Someone who had listened in college when his family was far away, given advice, and helped do what he could to set him on the right path. The man inside the coffin had been a powerhouse of humor, good stories, energy and dynamism. A kind man. A kindred spirit.

He thought of silence—the silence of eight years, when his life had taken him away from that old friend and sent him off to start a career, a family, a life far removed from those college days.

Adam should have sent a card. Many cards. And letters. And called him every month, especially during the years after the old man had been forced to retire, victim of the degenerative illness that eventually killed him.

But he hadn't.

Silence. What kind of silence had it been? He wondered. Grace had spoken of hours without speaking, of comfortable silence.

Could a comfortable silence last eight years?

If he'd sent cards, written letters, called, would they have picked up right where they'd left off? Would his friend have understood?

Adam sat for a long, long time in the dim room, and the silence drew out, lengthened, like shadows in a late afternoon.

Then he started talking.

On the Edge of Twilight

At least half the time, when the young man walked briskly through the park at twilight, he saw the old man sitting on the bench beneath the oak tree. And every time the old man was there, he called out to the young man and asked him a question.

And the young man sometimes stopped and sometimes continued on without bothering to answer, but the question, and the answer (when it came), were always the same:

"Have you seen the ghost?"

"No."

And then the young man was gone, gone to meet the girl he loved at their special spot. Or they were already together, walking hand in hand, to sit for a moment before going on to dinner, a movie, or someplace private to explore their love in new, breathless ways.

Neither knew what happened when they left the old man, and neither thought much of him; when their thoughts strayed to him and his strange question, they only focused on those things for a little while before excitement or happiness or a combination of both drew their attention away.

Both attended high school across the river. Both were seniors. They had been together, inseparable, for a year and a half. And in that time their routine on weekends, when the weather allowed, always included the park.

When they came together in the fading half-light she always slid her hand into his, either before they began to walk or when they met at their bench—always empty, as if waiting for them. The path to their bench led through the fields bordered by hedges and trees, past the old man's spot, through a gate, then finally down to the edge of the river, its shifting waters reflecting distant lights of houses on the far shore.

And when they chose to remain there instead of venturing out for the evening, they sat for hours, sometimes talking, often in murmurs, and night fell upon them and they came to life, focusing on each other with words and without, while staring at the river and the moonlight, and feeling rain and wind or stillness against their skin. Fireflies blazed around them in the summer-scented air. They rarely saw other people besides the old man; the park was old and difficult to find, and perhaps no one wanted it anyway. And then she would take his left hand again, threading her fingers through his, and he would put his right arm around her and pull her close, settling his cheek against the side of her head so he could smell her perfume and shampoo.

Every so often he would kiss her neck, and she would rub his knee, and they would shift their bodies so they touched in different ways. Then eventually, always, they found the rhythm of the night, and were lulled by it, and closed their eyes, drifting into a doze through the comfort of their attraction and the culmination of their surroundings.

And sometimes shortly after midnight, often not until several hours past, they would rouse each other, move into each other, run their hands over each other, whispering, kissing, sighing, before finally standing, walking, leaving their spot and returning to the world where other people lived and their love continued, but in the ebb and flow of an active world.

And the young man often thought, by day and at night, that he was fortunate, so fortunate, to have found someone who cared about him like she did, who understood him like she did, who loved him like she did.

Early on in their final year of high school, they spoke of attending the same university, and applied to several local schools together. But then, as the autumn progressed, they came to an obstacle. She was accepted to a university in California. He was accepted to a college in Maine. They were good schools, *excellent* schools—perfect for their interests and far better than those they might attend together. So they accepted the invitations, figuring a long-distance relationship would work, that they would *make* it work. And so they settled back into the comfort of their routine and didn't think of it.

Or said they didn't. For as the young man ticked off the days on his calendar and their 18th summer approached, he began to worry they would eventually be swept apart by time and circumstance and the need for something more—swept out of each others' lives forever, never to return, because perfection is fleeting, and elusive, and always becomes a thing of the past.

So he lived in the present more than he ever had in his life. Instead of looking to the future, he embraced where he was, when he was, who he was with and how he felt. *Healthy*, he thought. *It's healthy to do that.*

He told her that once, when the future weighed heavily upon them and she, too, suddenly became sad. And she agreed with him, and her mood brightened, and that was the last they ever spoke of it.

Once, out of the blue, when they were holding hands and looking out over the river, the bench warm and comfortable beneath them, she said abruptly, "I will never meet anyone else like you. And if I meet someone who is half the man you are with me, I think I could be content."

He nodded, took it only as a compliment, and chose to ignore the deeper implications.

Until suddenly the future became the present, and they were done with high school, graduation two months a memory, the cross-country moves in opposite directions just a day away.

At their spot, sitting on their bench, they said they would write, and keep in close touch, and see each other several times a year, but he knew it was all over, and he knew she knew it, too. And when true night fell and midnight knelled, the dark beginning of a new day, everything they shared retreated into the past.

They stood up from the bench for the last time.

She left quickly. He lingered a long while.

Eventually he walked slowly back toward the street, where his car waited in the shadows of the trees.

But he didn't go to his car. At the last moment he changed direction, instead approaching a second bench, the distant bench where the old man often sat in silence. He was there now, still awake; his watery eyes gleamed in the faint sliver of moonlight.

"I've seen you many times," he told the old man. "Why do you always come here?"

The old man looked up at him. "I wait for the ghost," he said simply.

"Is this place haunted?"

A nod.

"What does the ghost look like?"

"Different things to different people."

He gazed at the old man, then peered toward the dew-covered fields, the lengthening moonlight shadows, the cold river.

"Have you ever seen it?"

The old man nodded.

"How many times?"

"Every night."

The young man paused, blinking rapidly. "Mind if I join you?" he asked.

The old man looked surprised. "No… but why would you want to?"

The bench creaked under new weight. The old man slid over a fraction of an inch.

"Because I want to see it, too."

And the sliver of moon began its inevitable descent.

Supper-Time

"Get in here, Hank. No use turning my hallway into a wind tunnel."

Henry McMurran limped in with a grunt and shut the door behind him with a tremulous hand, cutting off the frost-flecked breeze and stomping slush from his galoshes.

Simon Farber led the way back to his kitchen, cane tapping the worn linoleum. "One lump or two?" he asked over his shoulder.

"In all my years, have I ever taken sugar?"

"Always a first time."

"And don't ask if I want milk, neither."

Strong coffee met chipped mugs, and the two old widowers creaked down in their chairs at the scarred kitchen table, fixtures in the room as much as the decades-old stove, hand-cut cabinets, and fly-specked overhead light.

Farber observed, simply, "Cold outside."

"How would you know? You got to go *out* to see what the day's like, you old recluse. You even know what month it is? What *season?*" Hank grinned, then grimaced. "Damn, this coffee's hot! Make the devil himself wince."

"Stop your whining. Mine's better than yours and you know it. And I don't go out because there's no good point."

Silence followed—the quiet of old friends who, after 75 years, don't need to talk in order to feel comfortable in one another's company.

Finally: "I had a dream last night, Simon."

Farber set down his cup. "I guess you'll have to tell me all about it, then. You always do."

McMurran leaned forward, elbows on the table. "This was an odd one. Left me feeling… strange."

Farber raised his eyebrows, waiting.

"I was here, in Still Creek, but the old Carnegie Library was still standing and Main Street was still dirt. The cars? Model-Ts. And the great old oak tree that stood in the square... remember it? Struck down by lightning in 1951? Yeah, that was there, too."

The mildly amused gleam in Farber's faded gray eyes disappeared.

"Hank," he said softly. "Was it summertime?"

McMurran looked up sharply. "Sure was. *Middle* of summer, I'd guess. Maybe a week shy or a week late of Independence Day."

"And," continued Farber, his whisper now just the faintest breath of stale air, "was *I* there, too?"

McMurran took a fast, deep swig of scalding coffee. This time he didn't even wince. His answer came as if blown into the room on a far-away wind. "Yes."

"And we were young."

"Twelve, I guess."

Farber nodded. "And we went fishing with our split-bamboo rods down at Cobblestone Creek outside town, in the hollow where the water's deep and the swinging rope used to hang from the willow tree."

McMurran's mug dropped from his hand to shatter, unnoticed, on the table. "What else?"

Without hesitating, Farber replied, "Margaret Pendergast was there, and so was Bud Collins, and his little brother Jake... Oh, and—"

"Johnny Saxon," McMurran finished. "Jesus, Simon, what's *happening*?"

Farber flashed an odd smile. "I haven't the foggiest idea, you nutty old coot. But I *like* it. Now clean up your damn mess."

* * *

That night, with the wind howling through the eaves and snow falling thick and heavy on every rooftop, road, and lawn across town, Simon Farber lay beneath crisp, clean sheets and his favorite old quilt and tried to sleep.

Across the street, he knew, Hank McMurran was already unconscious, probably in his overstuffed chair by the fireplace. The man could fall asleep during an earthquake, nod off in a flood. Anticipation didn't faze him and neither did novelty. Only death scared him, and so he avoided beds, icons of hospitals and illness, diminishment and frailty.

And Farber himself? The only thing that scared him was the world outside his house—the looming, teeming world that had struck down his wife with a car four years before, then continued spinning, as constant and oblivious as ever, toward other destructions.

He sighed, and his thoughts shifted back to the dream.

Would it come again?

Farber moved slightly. Arthritis shot pain through his knee and into his hip, where it remained, pulsing to the beat of his heart.

I want to run, he thought, *but that's a luxury I haven't had in forty years.*

The thought a mantra in his mind, he rolled over, settled, finally closed his eyes…

…and awoke in a field of tall grass, warm sun blazing overhead, the sound of bumblebees and cicadas a constant, rhythmic drone.

He sat up, looked down at his body, then leapt to his feet.

He ran.

Dandelions exploded beneath his sneakers. Milkweed pods broke against his legs. "Hey!" he cried, spreading his arms. "Hey, I'm a bird, I'm an *airplane!* Hey!"

"You're a nut."

He turned.

"Hank! *Look* at you!"

"Look at *you!*"

"I… It's… I'd *forgotten what I looked like!* It was like a movie, like another person, like something in a *book*."

"What?"

"My childhood."

Hank smiled, his two front teeth still ridged nubs. "We were here yesterday."

Simon's mouth worked for a moment before he could speak. "I didn't *know* then," he said finally.

"Know what?"

"That it wasn't only in my mind."

Hank nodded. "You remember this place?"

"Blaze Field, past the fishing hole on the other side of the creek!" Simon motioned with a lean, tanned arm. "Town's that way!"

And Still Creek was just as it had always been—before the mines closed, the sinkholes opened, the strip malls shut the shops, and half the town moved away. The Model-Ts, the good brick buildings with lead-glass windows, the plank sidewalks, and Quigley's wooden-floored drug store…

And it was there that they found Margaret Pendergast sitting on a tall stool at the counter, sharing a root beer float with Johnny Saxon.

"No one here to help us, guys," said Johnny. "So we helped ourselves. C'mon, have a malt!"

Simon scratched his head. "Yeah, where is everyone, anyway? It's a ghost town! Just us and the empty streets."

At that moment Bud Collins stumbled in. He looked eagerly at the other children, then his face fell. "I can't find my brother," he said, slumping into a booth. "I thought he might be with you."

They clustered around him. "Maybe Jake's not asleep yet," said Margaret.

Bud shook his head. "You don't know?"

"Know what?"

"What, Bud?"

"He died yesterday afternoon. Cancer. Had it for years. And I thought, you know, that maybe he'd still be *here*."

Silence. No one could think of anything to say. Then Bud got up, went behind the counter where Mr. Quigley used to serve ice cream and malts, and made himself a banana split; the icebox was frosted and fully stocked.

"I'm sorry," Hank said at last. "He was a great fella."

Bud nodded. "It's strange… I *feel* him near, but I can't find him." He took a bite of ice cream and banana, then another, until the whole thing was gone. At last he smiled. "Well, Jake never liked too much mourning and maudlin talk, so I'm done. Wanna go swimming in the quarry?"

They did.

* * *

Every night for the next two months, Simon joined his friends in the young town, in an old time, but they never saw Jake. While awake, it was winter and he felt it in his bones. Asleep? Summer. Every evening as his wispy hair touched the cool, white pillow, he anticipated it. And every night he played in the empty town of his youth with his four old/young friends in the blazing sun of an early-July day.

"Strange," Hank said in Simon's kitchen one icy morning in mid-February.

"Hmm?"

Hank eyed his coffee disdainfully. "This is awful. Strange, I said. We always wake up when it's getting on toward evening in our dream, right? Just as the fireflies are coming out?"

Simon nodded.

"Well, last night, as the sun began to set and the dream began to fade, I *swear* I heard a voice calling my name."

"A voice?"

"Yep. And what's more, I *knew* it."

"Who was it?"

"I'll give you a hint. When it came, we were five doors down from my old house."

Simon paused, thought, then said, "But Hank, we were *in* your folks' house earlier. No one there! Just like everywhere else. Food in the pantry, lemon pie on the windowsill, toys in your room, but no people."

"Doesn't matter. It was my mother. I haven't heard her voice in sixty years, but I'd know it anywhere."

"What did she say?"

Hank cleared his throat. "She was calling me home for supper."

"I don't understand." Simon sighed. "An empty town, phantom voices..."

"Simon."

He looked up. Hank's face was set, like he had something he wanted to say. Then it relaxed. "Gimme some more of that rotten coffee, huh?"

* * *

They were catching the first fireflies in the growing dark with Margaret, Johnny, and Bud when it happened. Hank snapped his head up, eyes wide, and dropped the Mason jar. Two-dozen glowing pinpricks rose up in the air around them and flooded the sky.

"You hear it?" Hank demanded.

Everyone stopped. Margaret shook her head.

"None of you? Clear as a bell!"

Hank started for home.

"We'll wake up soon," said Simon, trotting along beside him. "We always do before full dark. You won't make it."

"Yes, I will."

"But—"

"Simon," Hank said, his young face very serious, "there's something for you under your welcome mat. I put it there before I went to sleep."

"But Hank, I don't—"

And then the world began to spin, time shifted, one season intruded upon another, and Simon woke to another dark, winter morning in his still, quiet house.

He breathed deeply, cocooned in his quilt, then remembered, limped downstairs, opened the front door, hissed as the cold air hit his face and legs, and stuck his hand under the mat.

The note was short. It read:

No more bad coffee, Simon. Heart's been aching for a week, and worse tonight.

These last few months have been a gift. Why, or from whom, doesn't matter. And we both know the same gift means different things to different people. For me, it was the chance to get ready for what I knew was coming. For you, it's something else entirely. I'm sure of it.

Ain't that grand?

I'll be waiting to play Kick-the-Can when the time comes. Always was better at it than you.

Call Blake's Funeral Home if you get this.

The breath woofed from his lungs. Numb hands dialed 911.

* * *

"I'm sorry, Simon."

They sat beneath the old oak tree in Still Creek Square. Margaret placed a gentle hand on his shoulder. Johnny blew his nose. Bud remained silent, brooding.

"He said he'd be here," Simon said. "He said he'd be waiting to play."

But he wasn't. And in the days that followed, Simon Farber turned further in upon himself, by day a quiet old figure in his cold winter house, by night a boy who thought more and played less in the warm summer sun.

"I wonder," Bud said some weeks later, light reflecting off their favorite fishing hole in a shimmering veil, "why we're always here by *day*? Never night. Night was my favorite time during the summer." He laughed. "Still *is*. And it was Jake's, too."

Simon nodded. A trout nibbled his line but didn't bite. "I guess we all felt that way." Off in the distance, Johnny was teaching Margaret how to throw a football.

Bud, always the quiet one, continued, mouth a rare fount of words: "Remember? We'd go in for supper, eat as fast as we could, then meet by the baseball diamond at the end of the street. Half a dozen, ten, a dozen of us! You and me and Jake and Johnny and Hank and Bill and Travis and Davy… even the Moeller twins! And if we didn't want to play, we'd race downtown and all the stores would still be open, the street lamps blazing, and Preston's barber pole all lit up, and we'd go to Quigley's for a malt and some penny candy then rush off to the State for the late-night feature. The whole town would be alive—young couples courting, old folks on porches, dogs in the park, little children chalk-drawing on sidewalks. Or sometimes, if we didn't have money, we'd eat homemade ice cream and head outside for a game of—"

"Kick the Can," Simon finished. He looked up at Bud and smiled. "That was always Hank's idea… his favorite. It was a game for the evening, when our dads could join us if they were feeling young and we could see the glint of tin in the dark. Always late in the day. Always…" He paused.

"Always after supper," he finished slowly.

Bud nodded. "Jake heard someone calling, too. The day before he died. Just like Hank. Know what I think? We're the last living people from the town of our childhood. And you know what else?"

Simon looked at him closely. Suddenly, surprisingly, he thought he did. Bud didn't even need to say it.

Hours later, in the early evening half-light, he stood before his old home—long demolished but now whole again, wrap-around porch freshly painted, wicker swing creaking softly in a warm wind—and waited.

Nothing. No voice. No feminine hand and summer-green sleeve pushing the screen door open to venture out into the heat. No familiar but long-lost face to look first up the street, then down, before calling, calling, calling so that wherever he was, he'd hear, then come…

"A bit longer, I guess," he said softly. "Sometime soon. But for now…"

He looked up at the sky. "Fifteen minutes of daylight left. Still enough for a little fun."

* * *

And when he woke up to the bright sunshine of an early March morning, Simon Farber went downstairs, wincing as his arthritis complained, and stepped out on his front porch, surprised to find the snow melting and a warm breeze heating the air.

"A good day to go out," he murmured.

Stepping carefully down onto the sidewalk, he began to whistle. His young neighbor, Dan Preston, called out, "Good to see you about, Mr. Farber! What's up?"

"Oh, just enjoying the day," he replied. "They go so fast, you see. And then, before you know it, it's supper-time."

"My favorite meal!" Preston exclaimed.

"Mine, too. It's nice to know it's always there, waiting for us. But in the meantime… what a beautiful day for a walk."

Simon Farber tipped his hat. Whistling again, he continued on down the street.

About the Author

Gregory Miller was born in State College, Pennsylvania in 1978. His work has appeared in over 50 publications, and most of his fiction is collected in this book, along with his previous two books by StoneGarden.net Publishing, Scaring the Crows: 21 Tales for Noon or Midnight and The Uncanny Valley: Tales from a Lost Town. A high school English teacher for over a decade, he lives in Pittsburgh with his family, where he is currently working on a prequel to The Uncanny Valley. Miller welcomes comments and feedback through his website, http://authorgregorymiller.wordpress.com/.

About the Illustrator

John Randall York was born in Tyler, Texas and grew up playing and working in a small zoo where his father was the director. He loves ghost stories, old horror movies, and illustrations from the middle 20th century. He also enjoys writing songs and playing guitar.

In addition to On the Edge of Twilight: 22 Tales to Follow You Home, John has illustrated The Uncanny Valley: Tales from a Lost Town, Scaring the Crows: 21 Tales for Noon or Midnight, and the cover of The Sounding of the Sea: Five Tales of Loss and Redemption, all by Gregory Miller. Mr. York recently wrote and illustrated his first children's book, King Bronty, also published by StoneGarden.net. His artwork is available on his website, johnrandallyork.com.

He currently lives in Tyler, Texas with his wife and three cats.